Jaguar

By the same author
THUNDER CAVE

Jaguar

ROLAND SMITH

HYPERION BOOKS FOR CHILDREN
NEW YORK

For Marie, as always . . .

Printed in the United States of America.

First Edition

1 3 5 7 9 10 8 6 4 2

This book is set in 14-point Perpetua.

Library of Congress Cataloging-in-Publication Data
Smith, Roland, (date).
Jaguar / Roland Smith. — 1st ed.
p.   cm.
Summary: While accompanying his father on an expedition up the
Amazon River to a jaguar preserve in Brazil, fourteen-year-old Jacob
must contend with dangerous animals and fortune hunters.
ISBN 0-7868-0282-0 (trade)—ISBN 0-7868-2226-0 (lib. bdg.)
[1. Rain forests—Fiction. 2. Jaguar—Fiction. 3. Adventure and
adventurers—Fiction. 4. Amazon River Valley—Fiction. 5. Brazil—
Fiction.] I. Title.
PZ7.S65766Jag   1997
[Fic]—DC20   96-36750

Contents

BEFORE . . .

I walked into the den. Pinned up on the wall was a huge map of the Amazon Basin in South America. On the floor were stacks of books, scientific journals, and my father—a field biologist named Robert Lansa, Ph.D., also known as Doc to his friends and to his only son.

Doc sat in front of a laptop computer, staring intently at the screen. He didn't notice I was there. I was used to this.

"What's going on?" I asked.

He grunted and didn't look up.

"What's with the map and stuff?"

"Brazil, field project, preserve, jaguars," he mumbled.

When my mom was alive, she called this kind of response, "Lansa Latin." It had been awhile since I had heard this language. My mom's technique for dealing with it was to leave my father alone and wait for him to snap out of it. I left the room.

I went into the kitchen and opened the refrigerator.

1

Jaguar

Inside was a carton of sour milk, a block of cheddar cheese with splotches of green fuzz colonizing it, and a new item—a half-empty jug of orange juice. My father must have decided to go on a health kick. I grabbed the OJ and rinsed out a cup from the sink, which we were using as a cupboard.

Translating my father's mumbling was easy. He was looking at a field project that had something to do with a jaguar preserve in Brazil.

The only thing that surprised me about this was the timing. We had only been back in the States for a few months, and the tan I got in Kenya hadn't totally faded yet. We had rented a small house in Poughkeepsie, New York, near my grandfather's retirement home. His name is Tawapu, but we call him Taw. He's a Hopi Indian who spent most of his life riveting steel girders together high above the streets of New York City.

The plan was to stay in Poughkeepsie for at least a year while my father wrote up his research notes on elephants and got them published. It looked as if the plan might change, which was fine with me. Poughkeepsie was an okay city, and I liked the high school I was going to, but after my trip to Kenya, life was a little too tame for my liking. A trip to Brazil would be fantastic!

I waited a couple of hours, then went back into the den. My father was on the phone talking to someone. When he saw me, he covered the mouthpiece.

"Hey, Jake," he said. "I'm going to be hung up here for a while getting this together. I'll tell you all about it when I have it figured out."

This was polite Lansa Latin for "Get out of the den and don't bother me." I nodded and closed the door.

I didn't see my father for several days, but he left signs that he was still alive. I'd get home from school and find human spoor like pizza boxes and coffee grounds on the counter, and every once in a while I'd hear him talking on the phone behind the closed door.

Late on the fourth night he finally emerged from his den. I had just put away my homework and was getting ready to go to bed.

"Hey, Jake," he said. "Shouldn't you be in school?"

"I don't go to night school, Doc."

He wandered over to the window and opened the blind. "Wow, I really lost track of time."

That wasn't all he had lost track of. His long black hair hung down to his shoulders without the benefit of the usual ponytail, and he hadn't shaved for a week. I couldn't tell if he had changed his clothes, because he always wore jeans and denim shirts. He had at least a dozen sets exactly alike.

He turned back from the window.

"You remember Bill Brewster?"

"Sure." Bill was one of my father's oldest friends. They

3

had spent a lot of time in the field together studying animals. I hadn't seen Bill since my mom's funeral.

"Well, he's in Brazil now, and he's looking for someone to help him set up a jaguar preserve down there."

"And that someone is you."

"Right." He paused. "I won't be gone long."

I stared at him. He hadn't said the magic word—*we*. "How long?"

He looked away—a bad sign. "Not long. A month. . . . Maybe a little longer."

I should have seen this coming. Doc had become increasingly distant over the past few weeks. He'd go out for long walks by himself and spend hours closed up in his den. Some days we didn't say more than a dozen words to each other. I thought he was just concentrating on his book about elephants and didn't have time for me. I realized, now, that it was something else.

"And what am I supposed to do?" I asked.

"It's not like I'll be gone forever."

He had said the same thing when he went to Kenya. I didn't see him for over two years.

"What about my flying lessons?" I had just taken my first solo flight. The plan was for me to get my pilot's license by spring so Doc and I could do some cross-country trips this summer.

He walked back over to the window and looked outside—not that there was anything to see.

"I talked to Pete over at the Home," he continued. "He said you're welcome to stay there until I get back."

"You're joking."

"It's not like it's permanent."

"I thought we were a team," I reminded him, as calmly as I could. "Partners."

He turned back to me. "We are! But you have school."

"I could take correspondence courses."

"It's not the same. And I'll only be gone a little while."

Doc had made up his mind, and I knew there was no point in arguing with him. He was the most pigheaded man on earth, which is one of the reasons he and my mom had broken up before she died. For some reason, Doc had now suddenly turned into a parent. Our partnership was dissolved.

"I'll just stay at the house," I said.

"You're only fourteen, Jake. You can't stay here by yourself."

"I was in Kenya by myself."

"That was different. In this country there are laws about leaving minors by themselves."

"I won't tell anybody."

"Knock it off, Jake. You're going to stay with Taw at the Home."

Definitely a parent.

"That isn't fair."

"I'll only be gone a month," he said. "Maybe a little longer. . . ."

The Home

CHAPTER 1

Taw's retirement home is about ten miles outside Poughkeepsie. Years ago it was a resort hotel. From the outside, it still looked like a hotel, but the image changed when you walked through the front door.

On the main floor was a recreation room with three televisions mounted on brackets hanging from the ceiling. The televisions were tuned to three different channels, and the volume was kept so loud you could hear the soaps and *Oprah* from the front porch. The recreation room also had several tables set up for jigsaw puzzles, cards, and board games. Along one wall was a small library with large-print books. Once a week the local library sent a van over to take the books people had read and replenish the shelves with new titles.

Next to the recreation room was a clinic. In the morning this was the first stop for the *inmates,* as some of the residents called themselves. Before breakfast they lined up for their little white paper cups of brightly colored pills. This morning ritual was called the M&M's—*morning meds*. The nutritionist even put me on M&M's, which consisted of a cup of vitamins—at least I hoped they were vitamins. Then the nurse checked our names off a list. If people didn't show up for their M&M's, an orderly was sent to look for them.

Next to the clinic was a cafeteria. Everyone had an assigned seat so the nurses could make sure they got their "special" meals. The inmates called the cafeteria McDonald's.

Because I was young, the nutritionist let me have almost anything I wanted. At first I took advantage of this. But after a few meals with my tablemates staring enviously at my plate, I asked the cook to make my food at least look like theirs.

Taw was happy to have me around when he remembered who I was, which was only about half the time. Sometimes he thought I was a staff member, and at other times he thought I was an inmate. One time he mistook me for a childhood friend on the Hopi Indian reservation in Arizona—that was an interesting conversation!

Aside from me, the youngest person in the Home was Peter Steptoe. He was a thirty-two-year-old nurse. Peter and I got along very well. He was also very fond of my grandfather.

I guess the Home was pretty nice, but you haven't lived until you've been marooned in a house with fifty surrogate grandparents. Everyone meant well, but they drove me crazy!

My daily routine never varied. I was usually up by six in the morning. After my shower I went down to the clinic, got my M&M's, then ate breakfast with everyone. After breakfast Peter drove me to school, because buses didn't run this far outside the city. After school, Peter picked me up and drove me back to the Home. I held what came to be known as the *Press Conference,* had dinner with everyone, did my homework, and went to bed.

The Press Conference came about because everyone wanted to know what I had done during the day. When I first got to the Home, I would tell anyone who asked about my day. Fifty times! It took hours. If I left anyone out, their feelings got hurt. Peter thought it would save me a lot of time and spare people's feelings if I told everyone about my day at one time. The Press Conference was held in the recreation room every evening just before dinner. I thought the other inmates would get bored with it after a few days, but they didn't. The televisions were turned off and the recreation room was always jammed. Here's how a typical Press Conference went:

ME: Well, let's see. . . . Peter dropped me off at school this morning. I went to my classes and every-thing went pretty well. In history Mr. Pentegrast showed us a video on the Vietnam War. We played volleyball in PE. My team lost. After school I spent some time in the library doing research on a paper I'm writing on the Amazon rain forest. Peter picked me up and drove me back here. That's about it for today.

[*Hands are raised.*]

ME: Mr. Blondell.

MR. BLONDELL: You saw the video on the Vietnam War. What did you think of it?

ME: It seemed like a tragic waste of human life and money.

ME: Mrs. Mapes.

MRS. MAPES: Didn't you talk to anyone at school?

ME: Well, sure I talked to . . .

MRS. MAPES: Who?

ME: Well, I talked to Patty Teters.

MRS. MAPES: What does she look like?

ME: I don't know. . . . She has brown hair, brown eyes, she's about . . .

MRS. MAPES: Cute?

ME: Well, yeah. I guess so. . . .

MRS. MAPES: You're too young to get involved with anyone. You have your whole life to . . .

You get the idea.

When I first got to the Home, I made a couple of mistakes. The first was doing my homework in the recreation room. I sat down at one of the tables and started to work on a geometry problem, and suddenly there were seven inmates surrounding me asking if I needed any help. My second mistake was saying, "Sure."

They all started helping at once. A disagreement broke out, which quickly escalated into a shouting match, and before I knew it, two of the old guys started swinging at each other. Peter rushed in and broke it up. He suggested that I do my homework in my room to avoid this happening again.

My room was on the second floor, just down the hall from Taw's. It was a nice room with its own bath and a good view of the stream that ran into the lake in back of the Home. The room had an adjustable hospital bed, a nightstand, a dresser, and an oak desk that had seen better days. Hanging above the bed was a cord with a button on the end of it, in case I had a medical emergency. Because the room was temporary, about the only improvement I made was to put up a map of the Amazon Basin.

Doing my homework in the room stopped the fistfights, but it didn't stop the disturbances. After the Press Conference and dinner I'd go up to do my homework. Usually, within ten minutes I'd hear a light tapping on the door: .

ME: Hello, Mrs. Bellows. What can I do for you?
MRS. BELLOWS: I know you probably get lonely here. I

just wanted you to know that if you need someone to talk to, I'm here.

ME: That's very nice of you. But right now I better get my homework done.

MRS. BELLOWS: Of course! I just wanted you to know that I'm here in case you need me.

ME: Thanks. I'll find you if I need to talk to someone.

MRS. BELLOWS: Wonderful! You're such a nice young man. Nothing like my own son, who only comes here three times a year to visit.

[*Ten minutes later another tap at the door.*]

ME: Mr. Clausen, what a pleasure.

MR. CLAUSEN: I hope I'm not disturbing you.

ME: I'm just trying to get my homework—

MR. CLAUSEN: That's why I'm here. I used to be an accountant. I'm a whiz at arithmetic, and I just wanted you to know that I'd be glad to help you if you need it.

ME: Thanks for offering. But right now I'm working on my geology.

MR. CLAUSEN: Hmmmm . . . I don't know anything about geology. But when you get to that arithmetic, I'm your man. I'm a whiz at that stuff. I really am!

* * *

It was the same every night—a constant parade of people dropping by. They meant well, but I didn't need any help—the homework was simple. What I needed was to be back in my own home with my father. Or better yet, I needed to be in Brazil. But I had a bad feeling this wasn't going to happen anytime soon. A month went by, and I hadn't heard a word from him.

Saturdays and Sundays were the worst. Peter was off on the weekends, so I didn't have anyone to drive me places. I could have asked one of the other staff members, but I didn't want to impose on them.

It was one of the worst winters in New York history. Two days after my father left, the snow started falling, and it didn't let up through most of February. The snowplows had piled it so high on the side of the roads that you felt as if you were driving through an ice cave. The lake in back of the Home and the stream that fed it were frozen solid. I made one trip out there and nearly froze to death. I hadn't gotten around to buying any winter clothes.

So on weekends I was stuck inside. I usually hung out in my room and read. When the door-knocking got out of hand, I took refuge on the second-floor landing.

The winding stairway leading to the upper floors was seldom used. It was off-limits for inmates unless they were accompanied by a nurse or an orderly. To get to the second and third floors, inmates had to take the elevator. Fortunately, this rule didn't apply to me. When I wanted to be alone, I'd go to the second-floor landing and sit in the window seat, which couldn't be seen from the hallway.

It had a great view of the stream and lake in back of the Home. Peter found me in the window seat one afternoon, reading a book.

"I won't tell a soul," he said.

The next time I retreated to the landing, I found a small reading lamp attached to the wall above the seat. Peter never said a word about it, but I knew he had put it there so I'd be able to use the seat during the evening if I needed to.

When I hid out on the landing, I could still hear people wandering the hallways looking for me.

"Have you seen Jake?"

"No, I was looking for him, too."

"I wonder what he's up to now."

"Heaven knows, but you know young people these days. You can never . . ."

It took me awhile, but I learned to ignore the searchers' voices and concentrate on my books.

Since Doc left, I had read everything I could find on the Amazon. Every week the library van brought me a new pile of books. I read about rain forest ecology, indigenous tribes, Brazilian history, insects, snakes, birds, mammals, and of course jaguars. Actually, there hadn't been a lot written about jaguars, despite the fact that they are the third largest cat in the world, right behind tigers and lions. This is because they live in very isolated areas and are extremely secretive—not unlike my father.

I also read books about the men who had explored the Amazon Basin. My favorite among the explorers was a man named Colonel P. H. Fawcett. In 1953 his papers and journals were published in a book called *Exploration Fawcett*. He spent his entire life looking for the fabled Muribeca gold mines, which some people thought were tied to an ancient civilization and its lost city.

Colonel Fawcett set out on his final expedition to find the lost mines in 1925, accompanied by his eldest son and his son's friend. No one ever heard from them again.

Another book I liked was by Sir Arthur Conan Doyle, of Sherlock Holmes fame. Apparently he and Colonel Fawcett were friends. Conan Doyle wrote a novel called *The Lost World*, which was loosely based on some of the things that Fawcett had seen and heard about during his various expeditions to find the Muribeca gold mines.

* * *

And this is how it went—M&M's, breakfast, school, homework, hiding, and no word from Doc. When he was in Kenya and I was still in New York, he would at least send me a letter once in a while to tell me he was okay. What was he doing down there? I knew he had a tendency to throw himself into a project and forget almost everything else, but this was the first time he had forgotten about me.

CHAPTER 2

By March, I'd had just about enough of the Home. More snow had fallen, and school was closed for a few days. The library van couldn't make it up the driveway, so there were no new books to read. The snow also kept the inmates' relatives away, which made everyone pretty gloomy.

The staff tried to cheer the inmates up by scheduling group games and theatrical skits, but the inmates weren't very enthusiastic.

Even Taw seemed depressed by our snowy isolation. He spent most of his time in his room looking through the spotting scope that Doc had given him for Christmas. I made it a point to drop by his room several times a day and see how he was doing. A couple of times I found him sitting in front of the spotting scope sound asleep, with his long gray braids dangling over his lap.

I was worried about my father. It wasn't like him not to

call or write. Peter guessed that the mail system in Brazil was not very good. "And the snow around here hasn't helped our own mail system," he said. He was probably right, but it didn't lessen my growing concern.

I started to think of ways to get down to Brazil. I had a valid passport, and with the credit card Doc had left me, I could buy a ticket. But there were a number of obstacles standing in my way. One of the problems was Peter. He was responsible for me, and there was no way he would let me go traipsing off to the wilds of Brazil. And if I ran away, he'd go out of his mind with worry—to say nothing of how this would affect the other inmates. I couldn't do this to them.

An even bigger barrier was the fact that I had no idea where Doc was. I knew he had flown to a city called Manaus, but he could be anywhere by now. When I went to Kenya to find Doc after my mother died, I at least had a rough idea of where he was. And what if I managed to fly down to Brazil and he was on his way back to the States?

It seemed that my only choice was to wait and worry. My mood swung between frustration and fury—frustration because there wasn't anything I could do, and fury at Doc for leaving me behind and not staying in touch.

One afternoon I got so fed up I just had to talk to someone about the situation. It was Saturday and Peter was off. My only choice was to try talking to Taw. There was only about a fifty percent chance that he would remember who

I was or hear what I had to say, but I didn't care. I was willing to try anything to get rid of the bitter thoughts stampeding through my head.

I knocked on his door. He didn't answer. I knocked again, then opened the door. As usual, he was sitting at his window looking through the spotting scope. He didn't turn around. I walked over and sat on the bed.

"I need to talk, Taw."

He still didn't turn around.

"I'm getting kind of frustrated living here and I'm worried about Doc. . . ."

I told him about everything that was bothering me. It must have taken me twenty minutes to get to the end. All through it Taw didn't move a single muscle in his thin body. He just continued looking through the spotting scope. I doubted he had heard a single word I said. He probably thought my speech was one of the shows on the downstairs televisions. Despite this, I felt a little better letting it all out like that. I got up from the bed.

"Nice talking to you, Taw."

I started toward the door.

"A buck."

I stopped and turned around. Taw was in exactly the same position. I thought for a moment that I was having an audio hallucination. Then I heard it again.

"A buck."

At first I thought he wanted a dollar. I didn't know why

he needed money. Sometimes it's simpler not to question my grandfather. I took out my wallet.

Taw moved away from the scope and pointed out the window. "Look."

I walked over and looked through the spotting scope. I put my wallet away, feeling a little stupid. A big buck—as in *deer*—was standing by a tree near the frozen lake. He was stretching his neck up to nibble on the last clump of leaves within reach.

"You should stalk him," Taw said.

"What?"

"Like you told me you learned in Kenya."

When I was in Kenya, I was taught to stalk animals by a Masai named Supeet. When I got back to Poughkeepsie, I told Taw about it. At the time I didn't think he was even listening. I hadn't thought about stalking since I got to the Home.

"That was different," I said, turning away from the scope. "For one thing it was a lot warmer and there wasn't two feet of snow on the ground."

"Wear warm clothes."

"In Kenya, I stalked without any clothes," I said. "I was naked."

"Too cold here," he pointed out. "You'll have to wear clothes. Perhaps all you need is a good stalk. I'll watch you through the telescope."

I looked through the scope at the buck again. He was on

the far side of the lake. A light snow was falling, blown by an east wind. I'd have to go around the lake from the west so I could come upwind of him. "It would take a long time," I said.

"I have plenty of time."

"I don't know how close I can get."

"You can try."

I went back to my room, put on white running shoes and three shirts, and grabbed my pillowcase. Next stop was the linen closet, where the nurses kept their laundered, white uniforms. I found a pair of Peter's pants and slipped them over the pants I was wearing. I put my coat on, then found a white lab coat big enough to fit over it. The next item was a pair of disposable surgical gloves, which wouldn't keep my hands warm but would camouflage them to some degree. The final touch was the pillowcase. I found a black marker and put the pillowcase over my head and made two marks over my eyes. I took it back off and cut out holes, then put it back on and looked in the mirror. I looked as if I was ready for Halloween.

The next challenge was to get out of the house without anyone seeing me in this getup. That was relatively easy, because one of the inmates was putting on a piano recital and everyone downstairs was in the recreation room listening.

It wasn't as cold as I thought it would be outside. In fact, when I began high-stepping through the deep snow, I started to get a little hot. I waved at Taw up in his window and hoped that he'd be able to keep track of me as I got closer to the buck.

My plan was to move at a regular pace until I got about 150 yards from the buck. As I made my way around the lake, I performed little experiments while I plowed through the deep snow. It was much more difficult than tracking in Kenya, because I had to lift my foot two feet in the air every time I took a step.

Before I began my true stalk, I stopped and caught my breath. The buck was on the other side of a large tree. If I moved slowly and kept the tree between me and the buck, there was a good chance of getting at least as close as the tree before the buck sensed me.

I started. One slow step at a time, like a blue heron walking in shallow water. At first my legs cramped, but I ignored the pain and eventually it went away. I got into the rhythm of the stalk—a zone where nothing mattered but getting to the buck undetected.

As I drew closer, I concentrated on the buck's ears. They were constantly moving, like twin radar dishes monitoring the snow-covered landscape for incoming threats. The nearer I got, the slower I moved. When the buck looked my way, I stopped in midstep, holding that position until he looked away and started eating again.

When I reached the tree, I stood behind the trunk. I was so close I could hear him pulling the brittle leaves off the branches. He wasn't more than six or seven feet away from me. I rested, then very, very slowly moved out from behind the tree. The buck stopped eating and looked directly at me, with his ears pricked forward. His nostrils flared, and I could see his breath. He didn't know what I was, or how I had gotten there.

"Trick or treat," I whispered and pulled the pillowcase off my head. The buck snorted and wheeled around on his hind legs. He bounded away with the underside of his tail sticking straight up in the air like a white flag.

I should have felt guilty for disturbing his meager winter meal, but instead I was ecstatic. I jumped up and waved the pillowcase in the air, hoping that Taw had seen the whole show. Knowing him, he probably dozed off halfway through, but I didn't care. As Taw predicted, the stalk had made me forget my problems for the first time since Doc had left for Brazil.

I walked back to the Home feeling great. It was nearly dark by the time I got there. Before going inside, I slipped off my wet running shoes and Peter's pants. I ran up the stairs to Taw's room to find out how much he had seen of the stalk. There were about thirty people crammed into his room and more people spilling out into the hallway.

"I couldn't see," Mrs. Mapes complained.

"We need more of them telescopes," Mr. Clausen said.

As I pushed my way into the room, people patted me on the back and congratulated me. Taw was sitting on the bed, smiling. In fact, everyone was smiling and laughing. It was as if the depression of the last week had been miraculously taken away.

"I invited a couple of friends up," Taw said.

"How much of it did you see?"

"We took turns," he said. "They let me look when you stepped out from behind that tree."

Marcy, the duty nurse, pushed her way through the crowd to Taw's bed. "I knocked on your door, Jake, and you weren't there. Then I came down here and discovered what you were up to." She reached into her pocket and pulled out a folded piece of paper. "This fax from your father came while you were out back."

I took the piece of paper. I didn't want to read it in front of the others. I excused myself and went down to the window seat and turned the light on.

Dear Jake,

Sorry I haven't written or called. It's been crazy down here, and I thought I would be coming back up there anyday, so I didn't get in touch. It looks like this is going to take longer than I thought.

There's an airline ticket waiting for you at Kennedy International Airport. The flight leaves on March 21 and returns on March 30. Just go to the Pan Am counter with your passport—you're on Flight 636 to Brasília. You'll have to spend the night in Brasília and catch the afternoon flight to Manaus. You can stay at one of the hotels near the Brasília airport.

    The only thing you need to do before you leave is to overnight your passport to the Brazilian embassy for a visa. I've contacted them and they'll stamp it and get it back to you before you take off. I'm sure Peter can give you a hand with this.

    We're looking forward to your visit. . . .

Love, Dad

Visit? The dates coincided with my spring vacation. It didn't sound as if Doc was coming home anytime soon. And it was clear that he didn't want me to stay down there with him.

Taw came down the stairs and joined me on the seat. I was surprised to see him on the stairs without a nurse, but I didn't say anything about it. Instead, I showed him the fax.

"We'll miss you," he said.

"I'll only be gone a week."

"When do you leave?" he asked.

"Next Saturday."

He looked at the lamp. "Is this working out for you?"

I stared at him. "Did you put this light here, Taw?"

He nodded.

"I thought Peter put it up for me. How did you . . ."

"Shhhh." He held his finger to his lips. "I'm not supposed to use the stairs without a nurse."

CHAPTER 3

The next five days moved like a glacier. . . .
On Friday I sat in my classes glancing at the clock every
ten minutes, imagining where I would be at that time on
the next day. After school, Peter picked me up and drove
me to the Home. The Press Conference that evening was
packed. The great buck adventure had renewed everyone's
interest in the youngest inmate. I didn't have much to say
about the day, but it didn't matter. What they wanted
to hear was the story about how I had learned to stalk
animals—for the fifth time that week.

They had a little celebration for me at dinner.
Mrs. Clausen made a cake and decorated it with a beautiful
jaguar. When we finished, Taw stood up to say something.
Everyone got quiet. He looked confused, as if he had forgotten why he was on his feet.

Mrs. Mapes came to his rescue. "What Taw wanted to say,

or suggest, is that you stay in touch with us while you're down there, Jake."

"Dispatches!" Mr. Blondell said. "You know, like correspondents sent back to the States during the Vietnam War. Reports about what's going on. When our son was in Vietnam, my wife and I were totally dependent on dispatches. Without 'em we would have been lost."

"I'm only going to be gone for a week," I said. "And I don't even know if there's a phone where my father's staying."

"There must be a fax machine down there," Mrs. Mapes insisted. "That's how your dad got in touch with you." She handed me a slip of paper with the Home's fax number scrawled on it.

"I'll try," I said. But I doubted Doc had a fax machine handy.

I went up to my room early, telling everyone that I needed to get ready for the trip. It took me less than three minutes to pack. When I finished, I lay down on my bed and thought about Doc. I played with the amulet I always wore around my neck. It was made out of a round, flat stone, about the size of a quarter. There was a hole in the middle and surrounding the hole was an intricately carved snake swallowing its tail. It had belonged to Taw when he was young. He gave it to my father and my father gave it to my mom when they got married. I'd worn it ever since my mom died.

I knew Doc wouldn't have sent for me if he were coming back anytime soon. I tried to come up with various schemes to convince him that I should stay down there, but I knew it was hopeless.

* * *

The next morning I was up before sunrise. Peter was coming to the Home at six to take me to Kennedy Airport. My plane didn't leave until eleven and it was only about a two-hour drive, but I wanted to make a stop on the way.

I took my bag downstairs and put it by the front door, then went into the kitchen to see if I could get something to eat. Peter got there about ten of six and joined me in the kitchen for some scrambled eggs and toast.

"Where's Taw?" he asked.

"Asleep," I said. "I thought about waking him and saying good-bye, but I didn't want to bug him."

Peter smiled. "When I talked to him yesterday, he said he was driving down with us to see you off. On the way back he's going to give me a tour of all the buildings he put together in the city."

"I'm sure he meant well," I told him. "But he probably forgot. He was supposed to give a speech last night and he forgot what he was going to say. He seems to be drifting more these days."

"He's sharper than you think. You better go up and check. He'd be pretty unhappy if we left him behind."

I went up to Taw's room and quietly opened the door. He was sitting in front of the window. As usual, he didn't turn around and he didn't say anything. I knew that when the weather got better, he would spend his days sitting by the stream, just watching it go by. He loved it out there.

I stood for a moment, looking at his long gray hair hanging loose over the back of the chair—the fact that it was unbraided meant that he had just washed it. Maybe he was planning on going with us.

"Good morning, Taw."

"My hair needs braiding," he said, without turning around. I couldn't tell if he was in a cloud or not. As far as I knew, he thought I was one of the aides or nurses.

When I was little, my mom showed me how to braid using Taw's hair. I got the brush, comb, and ties from the top of the dresser. I stood behind him and started combing his hair.

"How's your father?" he asked.

"I don't know. I haven't seen him for a while."

Taw nodded. I made a part down the middle of his head and started braiding.

"Not too tight," he said. "It gives me a headache if it's tight."

"Okay." I finished the first braid and wrapped a rubber band around the end. "I'm going to be gone for a week."

"Peter told me," Taw said. "I'm going to the city with you."

"I'm going to Brazil. Dad's setting up a jaguar preserve."

"I saw a jaguar once."

Probably at the zoo, I thought.

"It was in Arizona on the reservation. I was eight or nine at the time. A hunter had shot it."

I had read that jaguars used to cross the Mexican border

and wander into Arizona. But that was a long time ago, when northern Mexico still had a few jaguars.

"It was in the back of a pickup. The hunter came to the reservation to buy supplies at the store. He had his picture taken with the cat. I touched the jaguar. Its fur was beautiful and soft, but its body was cold and stiff. I thought about how wonderful it would be to see a jaguar alive in the mountains. But I never saw one. No one did."

"That's a great story, Taw."

He nodded.

"I'll miss you," I said.

"Brazil is hot," he said.

"We better go, Taw. Peter's waiting for us."

* * *

When we got to Brooklyn, Peter stopped at a florist shop so I could buy a bouquet of flowers. From there we made our way to the cemetery, stopping at the entrance to get a map so we could find my mom among the thousands of tombstones. The blanket of snow made everything look the same. It took us two complete passes before we found the right spot.

Peter parked his car as close to the site as he could and said he would wait. It was my third visit to my mom's grave.

"I'm going with you," Taw said.

"The snow's pretty deep, Taw."

Instead of responding, Taw got out of the car.

"There's nothing the matter with his legs," Peter said.

Peter was right. Taw had no problem slogging through the snow. When we got to the top of the small rise where my mom's grave was, he wasn't even out of breath. I decided that when I got back, we would go walking whenever we could. It would be good for both of us.

"There it is," I said.

I brushed the snow off the stone. When I saw my mom's name carved in the marble, the familiar lump lodged in my throat and I felt warm tears rolling down my cold cheeks. I split the flowers into two bunches and handed half to Taw. I planted my flowers in the snow. Taw smelled the flowers he was holding, then looked up at the sky.

"Mom's buried here."

"I know, Jake." Taw put his flowers next to mine. "I was thinking. When you come back, maybe we could go to Arizona. I'd like to see the reservation again. I'd like to go back home."

I stared at him. This was the most lucid he had been since I returned from Kenya.

"That would be great. I'd love to go there with you."

"I'll miss you," he said. "Try to stay in touch. It will mean a lot to everyone."

"I'll only be down there for a week," I said.

Taw smiled and put his hand on my shoulder.

When we reached the car, I looked back at my mom's grave. Her flowers were the only color on the snow-covered hillside.

Manaus

CHAPTER 4

I landed in Brasília late Saturday evening. In the crowded terminal, sweaty people pushed and shouted in Portuguese, which I didn't understand a word of.

Peter had booked a room for me at a hotel right next to the airport. I checked in, went up to my room, turned the television on, and fell asleep watching an episode of *Star Trek* in Portuguese.

The next morning I ate breakfast, then went back to the airport and waited for my flight, which left at noon.

When I stepped off the airplane in Manaus, the blast of heat nearly knocked me over. Breathing the air was like inhaling steam. By the time I walked the short distance to the terminal building, I was drenched in sweat.

A mass of people waited inside, holding up crudely drawn signs with last names printed on them. I tried to pick my father out of the crowd, but I didn't see him. I was just about ready to break through the throng and look for him in another part of the airport when I saw a sign that said LANSA. It was held by a man I had never seen before. He was tall, very thin, and completely bald. He wore wraparound sunglasses, a purple tank top, shorts, and sandals, and carried an old crumpled hat in his hand. On his left shoulder was a tattoo of a large blue butterfly. I read the sign again to make sure, then walked over to him, slowly.

"Are you Jake?" he shouted above the noise.

I nodded.

"Follow me." He turned around and started to wind his way through the crowd.

I wasn't sure if I should follow him or not. I turned around and looked for my father again. No luck. When I turned back, the skeleton with glasses was waving impatiently for me to come with him. I followed at a safe distance behind.

When we got outside the terminal, he stopped and put on his old battered hat, which looked as if he had done a headstand in a chicken coop while he was wearing it.

"My name's Buzz Lindbergh," he said, sticking out a hand embedded with years of black grease as permanent as the tattoo on his shoulder. I shook it, then asked him where my father was.

"He couldn't make it. He and Bill had to go downriver and pick up the boat. I expect they'll be back sometime tomorrow."

Hearing Bill's name made me feel a little better. Buzz was obviously connected with the jaguar preserve in some way.

"The limo is over here."

He saw my hesitancy and smiled. "I don't blame you for being a little leery. I don't think I would go with me if I didn't know me! Let's see how I can fix this up. . . ." He thought a minute, then continued. "Bill Brewster and your father have been friends since they were at college together. Your grandfather is named Tawapu—he's a Hopi Indian. He lives in a retirement home in Poughkeepsie, New York. You've been staying there since Doc came down here. You were with your father in Kenya last year. When you got back, you started taking flying lessons. Your . . ."

"Okay," I interrupted. "I'm convinced."

"Good. It's time to go to the warehouse."

"Warehouse?"

"You'll see."

He led me over to an old truck that didn't have a square inch of good metal on it. It was so rusty that the roof over the cab had corroded away, making a permanent sunroof.

"This is the limo?"

"Yep."

There were two boys sitting in what was left of the bed. Buzz pulled a couple of loose bills out of his pocket and handed one to each boy. They grabbed them and ran away.

"Manaus rule number one," Buzz said. "Never leave anything you want to see again without a guard. Two guards, if you can afford them. It's part of the economy down here. Kind of like insurance up in the States. Hop in."

Hopping in was easy. There was no door on the passenger side. I climbed up and sat down. Something sharp poked me. I jumped up and heard my pants tear.

"Sorry about that," Buzz said. "I should have warned you." He grabbed a clipboard off the dash and put it over the exposed spring. I sat back down, hoping I wouldn't get tetanus from the wound in my butt.

Buzz stomped on the gas pedal a few times, as if he were trying to squash a scorpion. "No key," he explained, reaching under the dash and sparking two wires together. The engine coughed, sputtered, then blew out a plume of thick black smoke. "No muffler, either!" he shouted above the racket. We lurched forward and passed a cheerful sign that said WELCOME TO MANAUS!—in several languages.

There was no point in trying to talk to Buzz above the noise. So I held on and tried to remember some of the things I had read about Manaus while I was at the Home.

Manaus is six hundred miles inland from the east coast of Brazil. It sits on the shores of the Rio Negro, close to where the Rio Solimões and Rio Negro join to form the Amazon River. The city was established by Portuguese colonists in the 1600s and was named after a tribe of Indians that lived in the region.

Jaguar

In 1839 Charles Goodyear discovered a way to turn the sap from rubber trees into rubber tires. This discovery turned Manaus into a thriving city in the middle of the jungle. The plantation owners, rubber traders, and bankers got rich from rubber exports and built palaces with their newfound wealth. They also built a beautiful opera house in the center of the city, and stars from all over the world traveled up the Amazon to perform there. It was said that some of the people in Manaus were so rich they sent their dirty clothes to Europe to be laundered.

This prosperity didn't last long. The British came in and managed to smuggle rubber-tree seedlings back to England. They cultivated the trees, then transported thousands of them to Ceylon and Malaysia and set up plantations of their own. The competition caused the rubber market to crash in Manaus, and people stopped sending their laundry to Europe. Manaus had been struggling ever since.

The first thing that surprised me about Manaus was the terrible air pollution. A visible haze of wood smoke and diesel fumes hung like fog in the humid air. My eyes watered as Buzz drove the gauntlet through the heavy traffic.

The streets of the city were packed with cars and motorcycles. The sidewalks were filled with people moving sluggishly through the late afternoon heat.

Buzz drove down to the waterfront, and we passed a huge marketplace. Gangs of children wearing ragged

T-shirts and shorts ran next to the truck with their hands out, begging for money. Dozens of black vultures perched on roofs and trees surrounding the market, waiting for food to drop on the ground.

We stopped at a chain-link gate, and Buzz jumped out and opened it. He drove through and stopped again.

"I'll get it," I told him, and closed the gate behind us.

He drove down a gravel road and stopped in front of a large warehouse, which had more rust on it than the truck he was driving.

"Home sweet home," he said.

A man in filthy clothes sat in a chair, leaning against the warehouse. He had an old side-by-side shotgun cradled in his arms. Buzz said something to him in Portuguese and gave him some money. The man glanced at me through bloodshot, unfriendly eyes, then walked away in the direction we had come.

"Another guard?"

Buzz nodded and slid open a wide, drive-through door. I stepped inside and staggered backward. The warehouse was hot enough to cook a pizza in, and it smelled like rotting fruit.

"I'll open the other side and we'll get a breeze going." Buzz disappeared into the dark interior, and a moment later a crack of broadening light appeared at the far end.

I walked further into the warehouse but stopped when something *plopped* on my head. I reached up to wipe it away, and my hand was smeared with smelly slime. "What the . . ."

"Can't you hear them?"

"Hear what?"

"The bats," Buzz shouted. "They're echolocating off the metal walls."

I listened and heard high-pitched *pinging* sounds echoing through the warehouse. The floor was covered with sticky bat guano. I glanced up, but it was too dark to see any bats in the rafters.

"I should have warned you," Buzz said. "You need to wear a hat in here." He opened a door along one of the walls and flipped a light on. "It's safe in our office."

On the way over, I got hit twice more.

"Wipe your feet before you come in." Buzz pointed to a mat outside the door.

"How many bats are up there?"

"You tell me."

Buzz turned a flashlight on and shone it at the ceiling. I looked up and my mouth fell open. I closed it quickly so something unpleasant wouldn't fall in. Every inch of the roof was covered with squirming little bats. There had to be thousands of them.

"Fruit bats," Buzz said. "We got a heck of a deal on the place."

"I bet."

"Come on in."

I stepped inside. Air-conditioning! It was probably seventy-five degrees in there, but it felt like the arctic compared to the warehouse.

"All the comforts of home," Buzz said.

I looked around. Along one wall were two sets of bunk beds. On the opposite wall there was a small kitchen, with a sink, refrigerator, and stove.

"We do most of our work in here."

"Good idea."

"I'll show you the rest of the place."

He opened a door near the sink and led me down a short hallway to a room about the same size. Satellite photos and maps of the Amazon Basin covered one of the walls. There were several workbenches with tools and radio telemetry gear to track animals. Buzz opened another door and showed me the bathroom.

"You might want to get cleaned up and change your pants."

I'd forgotten all about the tear in my pants. I felt back there and found that the rip was bigger than I thought.

"Yeah," I said. "Good idea."

I was irritated that Doc hadn't met me at the airport. He should have at least called and prepared me for Buzz. The only excuse I could think of was that there wasn't a phone nearby, or perhaps he had left town right after he sent me the fax at the Home.

* * *

I felt somewhat better after taking a shower and changing my clothes. I stopped in the map room and took a closer look at the gear and the maps. One of the maps had a large area marked in red. I assumed this was the jaguar preserve. It was a long way from Manaus. Buzz had said Doc and Bill were bringing a boat upriver. This probably meant they hadn't been to the preserve yet, which meant that Doc had been in Manaus for the past seven weeks, which meant that he could have called me if he had wanted to.

I walked into the bunk room to ask Buzz what was going on, but he wasn't there. I did find a phone and fax machine, though. I picked up the receiver. There was a dial tone. Doc could have easily called or faxed me. I started to get irritated again.

There was a window in the door leading to the warehouse. I cupped my hands around my eyes and looked out. It was too dark to see anything clearly. All I could see were piles covered with plastic tarps to protect them from the rain of bat guano.

I waited for about ten minutes, then decided to find Buzz. Before I left, I put on my baseball cap. The smell in the warehouse wasn't as sour as before, and the temperature had dropped by at least ten degrees.

I walked out the back door. About fifty feet away there was a boat dock sticking out into the Rio Negro. The river had to be half a mile across at this point. The murky gray water flowed slowly. On the other side was a line of green tropical vegetation. I walked around to the front of the warehouse. No sign of Buzz, and the truck was gone. I walked back around to the dock, then went inside to escape the heat.

I found some paper and wrote a dispatch to the Home. There wasn't much to say aside from the fact that I had arrived safely, Manaus was filthy, Doc and Bill were bringing a boat upriver, and the heat was unbelievable. When I finished, I slipped the sheet into the machine and dialed the Home's fax number. The dispatch was on its way. Why hadn't Doc done the same for me?

An hour later I heard the truck pull up, and a few moments later Buzz came in with both arms full of groceries. I got off the bunk and gave him a hand.

"Dinner," he said. "But before we eat, you need to come outside." He looked at his watch. "We only have a couple of minutes. Don't forget your hat."

I followed Buzz outside and down to the dock. The sun was setting, and it had started to cool down some. Buzz kept glancing at his watch, then at the warehouse.

"What are we doing?"

"Five seconds."

"What do you mean, five—"

"Now!"

Thousands of bats poured out through the warehouse door. The noisy black cloud flew right over us and headed across the Rio Negro. It took at least three minutes for the warehouse to empty.

"There will be a few stragglers," Buzz said. "But that about does it. They'll be back early tomorrow morning. You don't want to be in the warehouse when they leave or come back to roost. Your dad says they go out every night to fill up on fruit. Someday I'm going to design an ultralight modeled like a bat."

"What's an ultralight?"

"I'll show you tomorrow. Let's go in and fix some grub."

Buzz was a pretty good cook, and for someone as thin as he was, he had a huge appetite. When we finished eating, I asked him if Bill and my father had been upriver to the place marked on the map.

"Not yet," he said.

"What's their plan?"

"You'll have to ask them. They should be back tomorrow sometime."

It was clear he wasn't going to tell me anything about what was going on. I helped him clean up the mess in the kitchen. When we finished, Buzz got into his bunk.

"We need to get up before the bats flap back to their roost tomorrow morning," he said. "You better get some sleep."

A few minutes later he was snoring. I wondered if that's where he got the nickname Buzz.

CHAPTER 5

I slept pretty well, considering the rattling air-conditioner and my roommate's snoring. Buzz was out of bed half an hour before I was, making coffee and fixing breakfast.

"We better get moving," he said from the kitchen, which was ten feet from my bunk.

I sat up. "What are we doing?"

"I need a hand getting the Morpho out of the warehouse before the bats come back."

"What's a Morpho?"

"It's a beautiful butterfly," Buzz pointed at the tattoo on his shoulder. "As soon as you eat, we'll go out and take a look."

I didn't know why he needed my help with a butterfly or why it was in the warehouse. Maybe he was the project's bug expert. He sort of looked like a praying mantis. I got dressed and ate. When I finished, I followed Buzz out into the dim warehouse. We wove our way through the tarp-covered piles.

"What is all this stuff?"

"Supplies for the expedition," Buzz explained. "If Doc and Bill come back with a serviceable boat, we're in business."

If the truck was their idea of "serviceable," I had some doubts about them making it upriver very far. Doc usually had much better equipment than I had seen so far.

Buzz stopped next to an unusually large tarp. "Grab hold of the corner. I'll get the other side and we'll peel it back together. I don't want to get any bat crap on the Morpho."

I took ahold of the tarp and we rolled it back. Underneath was an airplane. Or what looked like an airplane.

The wings were made out of electric-blue fabric. In the front was a small engine with a single propeller. Just behind and below the engine was a single seat that was no more than eight inches off the ground.

"The Morpho's an airplane?"

"Well, your dad calls it a go-cart with wings. Bill calls it a kite with an engine. They're wrong. It's called an ultralight. I named it after the most beautiful butterfly in Brazil. Unfortunately, you don't see many morpho butterflies around Manaus, because the children catch them and sell their wings to tourists."

"How does it work?"

"Like an airplane! I designed it myself, and I'm rather proud of it. It carries a single pilot and has a range of about a hundred miles. It has a five-gallon gas tank and a cruising speed of fifty-five knots. It weighs 232 pounds when the gas tank is full. The aluminum frame is covered with Dacron. The reason I leave it inside is to keep it out of the sunlight. Too much sun will turn the fabric into blue toilet paper. I'd find myself trying to keep an aluminum ladder airborne."

"What are you using it for?"

"We're going to track the jaguars with it. On the ground we'll be lucky to pick up the radio collar signal from a few miles away. I've been running some tracking experiments in the Morpho, and I've picked up radio signals from as far as fifteen miles away. And of course, tracking by air is more accurate."

I had helped Doc track elephants, and I was familiar with radio tracking techniques. But when we were in Kenya, we had a real airplane, not some cloth-covered toy.

"So you're a field biologist?"

"Nope. I'm a pilot and an ultralight designer. I volunteered for the expedition. I've always wanted to see how an ultralight performed down in the tropics. Give me a hand. We've got to get it out of here before the bats come back."

I took hold of one wing, and Buzz grabbed the other. We pulled the ultralight through the door. It looked even more flimsy in the daylight. It was nothing like the airplane I was taking lessons in back in Poughkeepsie.

"Go ahead and sit in the seat if you want to," Buzz said.

I climbed in—or, more accurately, I crawled in. There was a control stick and a pair of foot pedals, but they looked

Jaguar

like something you'd see in a video game arcade. Buzz had
designed the cockpit to fit his long legs, and I could barely
reach the floor pedals.

The control panel had several instruments: a variometer,
which keeps track of vertical airspeed; an altimeter, so you
know how high you are; an airspeed indicator; compass;
tachometer; and a temperature gauge.

"What's this?" I asked, pointing to an instrument I hadn't
seen before.

"That's a global positioning system, or GPS."

"What does it do?"

"It tells you where you're at. When you hit the button, it
sends out a signal that bounces off the nearest satellite. It
gives your exact longitude and latitude. Once you know
that, you can put in the longitude and latitude of your desti-
nation and it will plot a course to get you there. I won't be
using the GPS to find my way home, though, because I won't
be that far away from the base camp. I'll use it to pinpoint
the jaguar's location. I'll show you the tracking antennas."

I climbed back out, and he pointed to the end of one of
the wings.

"I built antennas right into the wing struts here and on
the other side. Coaxial cable runs right down this tube. I
can attach my receiver to the panel and listen to the
jaguar's signal like I'm listening to a compact disc. When
I'm right over the top of the jaguar, I'll hit the GPS button and it'll give me the cat's longitude and latitude.

Takes all the guesswork out of it."

Buzz was very excited about this feature, and I'm sure Doc and Bill were, too. It would make tracking a lot easier.

"I also have a two-way radio, so I can stay in touch with the base camp." He went into the warehouse and came back out carrying a helmet. "Got this from the air force. Go ahead and try it on."

Because of the heat, I didn't really want to, but I slipped it on anyway because I thought Buzz would be disappointed if I didn't. I even flipped the tinted visor down for the full effect.

"Everything hooks up to the helmet," he said. "And I have a switch that toggles between the two-way radio and the telemetry receiver, so I can listen to one or the other."

I took the helmet off and looked at the landing gear more closely. It consisted of two small rubber tires under the fuselage and an even smaller tire underneath the tail.

"I'll replace the landing gear with pontoons when we get where we're going. The only reason I have the wheels on now is that it's easier to pull it out of the warehouse." Buzz glanced at his watch, then looked across the river. "Help me get the Morpho out of the way. Our furry friends will be returning any minute."

We pulled the Morpho further away from the warehouse. A few minutes later the bats started to fly in from across the river. It wasn't as dramatic as when they had left, because they were more spread out. But it was still impressive.

"Bill and your dad insisted that we work around the bats rather than get them out of there."

This didn't surprise me. Doc always thought of the animals first, before his own convenience or comfort.

"I'm going to take the Morpho up for a little spin and run some tests. I could use your help, if you have the time."

What a joke, I thought. "No problem."

"In the map room is a two-way radio. I want to see how far away I can get and still stay in touch."

Buzz squirmed his long body into the cockpit, put on his seat belt, then slipped the helmet over his head. He connected the helmet to the radio outlet, held his thumb up, then started the engine. He swung the Morpho around, pulled the throttle out to full power, and started toward the Rio Negro. It looked as if he was going to run right into the river, but just as he reached the shore, he pulled back on the stick and the Morpho was airborne.

I watched him fly around for a few minutes. The Morpho *did* look like a flying go-cart. Buzz circled over the river a few times as he gained altitude.

I headed back into the warehouse. They had enough supplies in there to last them for months. Doc wasn't just down here to help Bill "get started." I should have realized there was no way he would be satisfied living in Poughkeepsie, New York. He may have come down here with the thought of helping Bill, but he was part of the expedition now. Where did that leave me?

I went into the map room, found the two-way radio, and switched it on.

"Buzz to base . . ." the speaker crackled.

I keyed the microphone. "Base to Buzz."

"How am I coming in? Over."

"Loud and clear. Over."

"Roger. I'll do periodic radio checks during the next hour. Over."

"Roger."

"Out."

I spent the next hour looking through the stuff in the map room and telling Buzz that he sounded just fine.

"I'm heading back in," Buzz announced over the radio. "And we're going to have visitors soon. Your old man is about forty-five minutes out."

"Great!" I said. "I mean . . . roger."

I went outside to watch Buzz bring the Morpho in for a landing. He came in low over the water, flying very slowly. When he got over shore, he pulled the nose up slightly and the Morpho touched down like a butterfly landing on a flower.

Buzz was drenched in sweat. "Hot up there in the wild blue," he said.

"So you saw Doc?"

"Yep. He should be here anytime."

I helped him put the Morpho back in the warehouse and cover it with a tarp. He went into the bunk house to take a shower, and I went out to the dock to wait for Bill and my father.

About half an hour later, an old boat came chugging up to the dock. Bill Brewster stood on the bow, waving. He was much stockier than Doc and had kept his long black beard, despite the heat. Doc was in the wheelhouse steering the boat. When they were close enough, Bill threw me a rope, and I tied it to one of the cleats. My father shut the engine off and jumped down to the dock. He was wearing his denim uniform and had his hair pulled back in a pony-tail. He came over and gave me a hug.

"Sorry I wasn't at the airport," he said. "Duty called." He made a gesture toward the boat.

Bill joined us and clapped me on the back. "Hot enough for you, Jake?"

"Too hot!" I said, smiling. The smile was involuntary. I wanted to be somber and surly, so Doc would know I wasn't happy about the way he had treated me. But it was just too good to see him.

"You look good, Jake!" Doc said.

"A little pale," Bill added.

"It's been snowing in Poughkeepsie."

"I wouldn't mind lying down in a snowbank for a month," Bill said.

Doc looked tired, but he was in very good spirits. I hadn't seen him this happy in years. He was either very pleased to see me, or was just happy to be back in the field, or both.

"You call this a boat?" Buzz came up behind us.

"It's the best we could do," Bill said.

"Who's the captain?"

"We flipped a coin," Bill said. "I lost."

"Or maybe you won," Doc said.

"Good point! There are a few minor mechanical problems," Bill admitted. "But nothing you can't fix, Buzz."

"I'd like to remind you that I'm an aeronautical engineer. Not a grease monkey."

Bill laughed. "I stand corrected. But we still need you to fix this pile of junk."

"Then you can give me a hand with the tools."

"I'll give you a hand, too," Doc offered.

"Forget it, Doc," Buzz said. "No offense, but you're not exactly a mechanical genius. Bill and I can handle this ourselves. Anyway, you need to pick up Flanna."

Doc acted as if his feelings were hurt, but he knew as well as they did that he was a complete klutz when it came to anything mechanical. Bill and Buzz headed toward the warehouse to get the tools.

"Who's Flanna?"

"Flanna Brenna. She's our botanist. And she's probably a wee bit upset. I was supposed to pick her up yesterday. I think you'll like her."

"What's going on, Doc?"

"I'll tell you all about it on the way to pick up Flanna."

* * *

The truck was so loud we could barely hear each other. Doc drove us out of Manaus and up into the hills. The roads, if you could call them that, were terrible. The vegetation got thicker and greener the farther away from the city we got.

"Most of this is secondary growth," Doc shouted above the racket. "You don't see primary rain forest until you get way up the Amazon. And even then you have to hike in a couple of miles from the river, because everything along the shore has been cut at one time or another."

"Why do they cut it?"

"Firewood, lumber, settlements, oil, gold . . . You name it! They're gobbling up the rain forest big time."

We were in the truck for at least two hours before Doc finally came to a stop, at what looked like a dead-end road. We got out and looked around. There was no one waiting for us there.

"This is bad," he said. "Flanna must have gotten tired of waiting, so she went back into the forest. We'll have to go find her. Want to go for a hike?"

"Sure." I went back to the truck and drank some water from the jug had we had brought with us. Doc did the same.

"The trail's over here." He pushed through a stand of thick green vegetation. "It will open up when we get under the canopy."

It took us awhile to get through the tangle of plants. Doc went first. He didn't seem to be following any kind of trail that I could see, but I was confident that he knew what he was doing. He might get confused driving a car or walking in a city, but put him in the middle of nowhere and he could navigate like an animal that had lived there its whole life.

When we finally broke through the ground cover, we stopped and looked up. We were surrounded by huge trees. Their massive trunks were wrapped with thick vines. The lowest branches were at least a hundred feet above us. Shafts of sunlight battled their way through the canopy to the ground, which was much more open than I had thought it would be. The forest was filled with sounds of animals I couldn't see.

"It's like a cathedral," I whispered.

"That's a good description. This is the only untouched rain forest for a hundred miles. Relatively untouched—people are beginning to encroach on the outer edges. It's hard to keep them out."

We started walking again and continued until we came to a narrow stream. Doc sat down on a rotting log covered with a thick cushion of moss. I sat next to him.

"I guess I better tell you what's going on," he said.

I nodded. He unlaced his boots, peeled his socks off, and let his feet dangle in the water.

"I'm not exactly sure where to begin."

"Why don't you start by telling me about the jaguar project?" I suggested, trying to make this as easy as possible for him.

"It's Bill's project, not mine. I just came down here to help him get it started. It's a little more involved than that now."

Translated, he was much happier down here than he was in Poughkeepsie and he didn't want to go back.

"Bill has been trying to put together a jaguar preserve for over twenty years. And it looks like he's about ready to pull it off. Just a couple more hurdles."

"Such as?"

"It boils down to this. There's a rich industrialist from the States who's getting a million acres from the Brazilian government in payment for a debt they owe him. His name's Woolcott."

I'd heard the name before. He owned an oil company or something in the States.

"Anyway, Woolcott loves jaguars almost as much as he loves money. The government gave him his choice of million-acre tract of land. He has a dozen to choose from and two months to decide which one he wants—and, more important, what he wants to do with the land. He can either set up a preserve and write off the debt, or he can suck out every last resource in the million acres and leave behind a garbage dump. Of course his advisers are telling him to go for the garbage-dump idea. He'll get all his money back and probably a lot more.

"But Woolcott's getting older and he doesn't need any more money. This is where Bill comes in. Bill pitched him the jaguar preserve idea. Woolcott liked it. In fact, he liked it so well that he told Bill to pick one of the tracts of land right on the spot. Bill did."

"So what's the problem?"

"Bill picked the area without knowing if it would support jaguars. And the deal is that he has to show reasonable progress within two months or Woolcott will pick one of the other sites and suck it dry."

"How does he define 'reasonable progress'?"

"Woolcott's been kind of vague about that. We know he wants radio-collared jaguars on the ground and enough tracking data to prove that the spot is a viable location for the preserve. In other words, the preserve has to be up and running within two months."

I thought about the terrible warehouse they were stuck in, the old truck they drove, and the decrepit boat they hoped would get them up the Amazon.

"Who's paying for all this?"

"Bill is. Flanna and I have put money in, too. We're on a pretty tight budget."

"Why doesn't Woolcott pay for it? He could probably fund the whole expedition with the change in his pocket."

"He says he's gone as far as his advisers will let him. If we show progress, he'll not only donate the land but set up an endowment fund that will pay for operating the preserve."

"So this is sort of a test or something?"

"That's one way of looking at it. Woolcott is pretty eccentric and impulsive."

Just like you, I thought. "Where does this leave me?"

Jaguar

Doc looked away. Not good. I felt the guillotine sliding down the greased grooves toward my neck.

"I'm not exactly sure," he said. "I mean, I've thought a lot about it. That's why I wanted you to come down here. I wanted to talk to you face-to-face."

We might as well get right to it, I thought. I took a deep breath. "I think I should stay down here with you," I said.

"I know." No eye contact. This was not going the way I wanted it to go. "But this isn't the best place for you to be right now. We don't know exactly what we're facing up-river, and it could be dangerous."

"I walked halfway across Kenya looking for you! I think I've proven I can take care of myself."

"You could have been killed in Kenya! I have enough on my mind without worrying about your safety. To say nothing of the fact that you have school."

I knew this excuse was going to come up. "Doc, I can't live in a retirement home until I go to college. It won't work."

"I know, I know. . . . I've been checking into some things. If you can just hang in there until the end of the school year, there's a summer camp in Colorado that—"

"What are you talking about?" I shouted, losing my cool completely. "I don't want to go to a summer camp. I want to be with you! How long are you staying down here?"

"I'm here for the duration," Doc said quietly.

"What's that mean?"

"I don't know."

"What happens in the fall after this so-called summer camp?"

"There are some good boarding schools. . . ."

I got up from the log and walked away. It was either that or start crying in front of him. How could he do this to me without even asking? What about what I wanted? I heard Doc call, but I kept walking. I'd figured I would lose the first round, but I thought I'd at least be able to spend the summer down here with him. He was talking about us being separated for a year or two! He was no longer helping an old friend out. This was as much his project as it was Bill's now.

Doc's voice got further and further away. He probably wished now that he hadn't taken his boots and socks off. Having to put them back on had given me a big head start. I found what looked like a trail and followed it. I had no idea where I was going, and I didn't really care.

Without any warning, something appeared right in front of me. Something large. I couldn't see clearly because my eyes were blurred with tears. I staggered backward, fell on my butt, turned over, and started crawling as fast as I could, back the way I had come. It had to be some kind of animal. Doc would be sorry now!

"I'm sorry. . . . I'm sorry. . . . I thought you were Bob."

I stopped crawling. Wild animals don't usually apologize before they attack you. Bob? It was a woman's voice. I turned around and looked. She had curly red hair sticking out from a yellow hard hat and was hurriedly undoing a climbing harness around her waist. Attached to the harness was a rope that was tied off up in the canopy somewhere. When she got untangled, she ran over to me.

"I'm so sorry. . . ."

I stood up and brushed myself off. "Who's Bob?"

"Aren't you Jake?"

I nodded.

"I was referring to your father."

My father, Dr. Robert Lansa, despised being called Bob. Everyone knew this. That's why he adopted the nickname Doc. When my mom was alive, he didn't even let her call him Bob.

I stared at the woman. She was about my height and had green eyes. She wore a pair of khaki shorts, a green sleeveless leotard, and a pair of heavy climbing boots. She had a slight but very athletic body. In other words, she was beautiful.

"I'm Flanna Brenna," she said.

"The botanist."

"Right."

I had a feeling that she was more than a botanist. I heard Doc running up the path behind me. He stopped when he got to us, slightly out of breath. Flanna smiled brightly when she saw him. He smiled back at her. She was definitely more than a botanist. I guess Doc forgot to tell me about this part of the expedition.

Jaguar

"I'm afraid I nearly scared your son half to death, Bob. I thought it was you. You look just alike from a hundred feet up."

"Jake, this is Dr. Flanna Brenna."

"We already introduced ourselves, *Bob.*"

CHAPTER 6

Flanna led us down the trail to her camp, which turned out to be 150 feet up in the canopy.

"I'll lower the gear down." She strapped her harness on, attached a rope hanging from a tree, and began her ascent, using some kind of clamping device that held her in place until she pulled herself up further. She made it look as easy as climbing a ladder, which I'm sure it wasn't.

I could tell that Doc wanted to explain the situation to me, but I was too mad even to look at him. I was convinced that Flanna was the main reason he didn't want me with him in Brazil. It had very little to do with how dangerous it was down here.

Flanna crawled around through the canopy like a monkey. Despite my feelings about her, I was pretty impressed with her abilities. She gathered her equipment and lowered it down to us one bunch at a time.

"Flanna has her doctorate in tropical ecology," Doc said.

"She's been down here for three years studying the medicinal uses of rain forest plants. She had a grant from a large pharmaceutical company in the States, but that ran out about three weeks ago. So she threw in with us."

I didn't say anything to him. Flanna must have come down here right after she got her doctorate. She was definitely under thirty, which would make her about fourteen or fifteen years younger than Doc. I had read about the medicinal uses of rain forest plants. Many of the lifesaving drugs we use originated from plants found in the tropical rain forest. Many scientists believe that the cure for almost every disease could be found in the rain forest. It was just a matter of finding the right plant before it was lost forever because of deforestation.

"Jake, I should have told—"

I interrupted him. "I don't want to talk about this right now."

"Okay," he said quietly.

"That's it!" Flanna yelled down to us. A few seconds later, she dropped from the canopy like a spider on the end of a silk thread. We each took some of the gear and headed out of the forest. I walked ahead so I wouldn't have to talk to either of them. I was angry and confused. I needed time to think—a lot of time. It was nearly dark when we got back to the truck. We put Flanna's stuff in the back and climbed into the cab. Flanna sat between me and Bob.

* * *

When we got back to the warehouse, we found Bill and

Buzz drinking beer and playing cards at the kitchen table.

"I see the crew is hard at work," Doc said.

"We need some parts for the engine, which we can't get until tomorrow," Bill said. "Pull up a chair, Doc."

"Not tonight."

"Flanna?"

"No thanks."

"That leaves you, Jake. You interested in joining our friendly little game?"

I was in no mood for cards, and watching them reminded me of my future with the inmates back at the Home. I shook my head.

"Flanna and I are going to walk into town and get something to eat," Doc said. "Anyone want to come?" He looked at me.

"I'm going to take a shower and go to bed," I said.

I found some clean clothes and went into the bathroom for a quick shower. When I came back, Bill and Buzz were still playing cards and barely noticed me. Flanna and Doc were gone. I walked outside and wandered down to the river.

It was a nice evening despite the humidity. Thick clouds had moved in, and lightning flashed on the other side of the river.

I thought of sending another dispatch to the home:

This afternoon my father told me he was sending me to summer camp. In the fall I'll be attending a boarding school. I had the pleasure of meeting his new girlfriend, Flanna Brenna. She's a knockout and young enough to be my sister. I hope things are well with all of you. Everything down here is absolutely perfect! Jake.

I tried to sort out my feelings. Doc and my mom had been divorced for a couple of years when she died. She remarried as soon as the divorce was final. The guy's name was Sam and he was a real jerk, but he and my mom got along pretty well. I put up with him for her sake.

Doc and my mom rarely got along. She loved living in New York City. Doc hated big cities—New York most of all. She was a professor and loved the university atmosphere. Doc thought university people were the most boring blowhards on earth. His idea of bliss was wandering around the middle of nowhere observing wild animals, or, as my mom used to say, "He's a man who needs to be out in the wilderness howling at the moon."

I didn't mind that Doc had a girlfriend. Flanna was obviously intelligent and independent, and could climb a rope better and faster than anyone else I had ever seen. What bothered me was the fact that he hadn't told me about her. After our experiences in Kenya, I thought he had become my partner. I thought that he had given up on being my parent. This is one reason he had insisted that I call him Doc, not Dad. I must have been mistaken.

Parents split up. Families split up. But partners stay together. Or so I thought. A partner should at least tell you when he finds a girlfriend. Doc was acting like a parent who didn't want to be a parent.

What was I acting like? I didn't want to think about this. I also didn't want to be in Manaus anymore. I couldn't stand the thought of five more days of Doc and Flanna having meaningful eye contact with each other. Five more days of knowing that I would be back in the Home in five more days.

Doc had the next few years of my life planned out for me. Three months of summer camp with other kids whose parents didn't want them around. Then off to boarding school, for nine months with kids in the same situation.

If Doc didn't want me with him, I guess it didn't matter how I spent the next few years. In the morning I would tell him that I wanted to catch the next flight back. No sense sticking around.

* * *

Flanna slept on a cot in the map room. The rest of us slept on the bunk beds. Well, I didn't exactly sleep. I spent most of the night lying on my cot listening to the others sleep.

I was grateful when Bill finally stumbled out of bed and started clanging around in the kitchen, trying to get the coffee going. I got up and helped him. Buzz and Doc weren't far behind. Flanna joined us just as Bill was pouring the coffee. She was the only one who looked relatively rested. Buzz and Bill were feeling the effects of their poker game, and Doc looked as if he had spent the night as wide awake as I had.

"So what's the matter with the boat?" Doc asked.

"I think it's the fuel system," Buzz said. "We'll take it apart this morning as soon as this coffee starts to work."

"When will we be able to leave?" Flanna asked.

"As soon as the boat's in shape, we're ready to go."

"We'll wait until next Sunday," Doc said, glancing at me.

"You don't have to wait for me," I said. "If you're ready to go sooner—"

"We'll wait," Bill interrupted.

"Actually, I was going to check and see if I can get an earlier flight back," I said. I looked at Doc. "I don't see any point in sticking around any longer."

This emptied the kitchen pretty quickly. Flanna remembered something important she had to do in the map room. Buzz and Bill took their cups of coffee to the boat to work on the engine. I think Doc wanted to go somewhere, too, but he didn't have any choice.

"I know you're unhappy with me, Jake—"

"You came down here knowing that you weren't coming back," I interrupted. "You put me in a retirement home, for crying out loud! You didn't write, you didn't call. You have a girlfriend who isn't much older than I am, and you're taking her up the Amazon and sending me back to summer camp and boarding school! I'm not unhappy, Doc. I'm furious!"

Doc glanced at the map room door. "Maybe we should go outside," he said quietly.

I wanted to suggest another place he could go all by himself, but instead I got up and went outside. Doc was right behind me. We went out the back door of the warehouse. Bill was just about to board the boat, carrying a gas can in one hand and his coffee in the other. Buzz was about twenty feet behind him carrying a heavy tool box.

"Okay," I said. "We're outside. Where do you want to go?"

Suddenly a blast knocked us both off our feet. Fiery debris slammed into the metal warehouse. I lay there with the wind knocked out of me as bats poured out through the open door.

After I regained my breath and some of my senses, I looked to see if Doc was okay. He was running toward the boat, now engulfed in black smoke. Someone was on the ground in front of the boat—on fire! I ran after Doc. I got there just in time to see his shirt ignite as he tried to help whoever it was on the ground. I tore my shirt off and wrapped it around Doc, smothering the flames. It was way too late for the other person.

I was afraid there might be another explosion. "Come on, Doc! We've got to get out of here!" I pulled him away from the boat.

"Who was it?" he screamed. "Who was it?"

I didn't know.

CHAPTER 7

It was Bill Brewster.

Buzz had somehow been blown free of the wreckage. His leg was badly broken, but he didn't have any burns. Doc's right hand and forearm were covered with ugly blisters. I was fine. Flanna and I tried to make Doc and Buzz comfortable while we waited for the ambulance and fire department, which seemed to take forever.

Flanna was very calm. She helped me get Doc into the air-conditioned kitchen and convinced him to lie down on the bunk and rest. Then we went back outside with a stretcher they had for moving tranquilized jaguars. We got Buzz onto it and carried him inside. Flanna told me to make Buzz as comfortable as I could. She went to work on Doc's hand and forearm, smearing on a salve of her own concoction. When she was done, she cut off Buzz's pant leg. The flesh was terribly discolored, and the leg was twisted at an unnatural angle.

Buzz lifted his head to assess the damage. "Looks like I

busted a strut," he said, then passed out.

"I'm afraid I don't have anything in my bag of tricks for a broken leg," Flanna said. "We'll just have to wait for the ambulance."

Only when she had done everything she could do, did Flanna break down. She held Doc's good hand and cried without making a sound.

The ambulance pulled up outside. I ran out and told the driver where we were. He and his partner brought a stretcher in. Flanna barked something at them in Portuguese, and one of them shrugged his shoulders.

"They only sent one ambulance," she said. "We'll take your father in the truck, if I can figure out how to get it started."

"I can show you," Doc said, weakly, and added, "Jake, you better stay here."

I was about to protest, when Flanna put a hand on my shoulder. "He's right, Jake. We can't leave our equipment untended. Every thief in Manaus will know we're at the hospital."

"Fine," I said.

"I'll call you from the hospital and tell you how things are going," Flanna said.

Buzz was placed on the stretcher and rolled out the door. Flanna and I helped Doc out of his bunk. He was in a lot of pain. Flanna managed to get the truck started as I helped Doc into the passenger seat.

"I'll be fine," he said.

I watched them drive away. The boat was still burning. Bill Brewster's body was hidden behind a veil of black smoke. I couldn't believe he was dead.

Suddenly a man walked out from the side of the warehouse.

"Can I help you?" I asked.

He stared at the burning boat. "Look's like you're the one that needs help."

He sounded like an American.

"What are you doing here?"

"I saw the smoke."

He had silver-gray hair cut so short it looked as if it had been painted on his head. His eyes were pale blue and his face was tanned and wrinkled, as if he'd spent many years in the tropics. He wore black jeans, white tennis shoes, and a starched white shirt. I guessed him to be in his late fifties, but he was in very good shape.

"What happened here?" he asked.

"Who are you?"

"My name is Jay Silver, but you can call me Silver. You must be Doc's son."

"Jake," I said. "You know my father?"

"Not very well," he admitted. "We only met once. So what happened?"

I had no idea what had happened. And I wasn't in the mood to have a conversation with a complete stranger. I was worried about Doc's injuries, and his best friend had just been killed. Who was this guy?

"The boat blew up," I said. "Bill Brewster's dead."

"And your dad?"

"His hand got burned."

"And the tall guy. I forget his name. . . ."

"Buzz," I said. "His leg's broken. They're at the hospital."

"You have no idea how this happened?"

I shook my head. "Bill and Buzz were going to do some work on the fuel system. But they didn't make it to the boat before it blew up."

"Did they work on the fuel system earlier?"

"I don't know. They were working on the engine yesterday. Why?"

"Things usually don't just blow up on their own. I'm just curious about how it happened."

A fire engine pulled up, followed by two police cars and a van. The firefighters got out of their truck, took one look at the fire, then got back in their truck and just sat there.

"What are they doing?"

"The cab's air-conditioned," Silver said. "I imagine they'll just wait for the boat to burn itself out. It's too late to save it."

A uniformed policeman got out of one of the cars and came over to us. He nodded at Silver as if he knew him, then started jabbering at me.

"I'll take care of this," Silver said, and launched into an

explanation in what sounded like perfect Portuguese.

The policeman took a pad out and jotted down some notes. When Silver was finished, the officer asked him a few questions, then saluted and walked back to his car.

Now it was my turn to ask what was going on.

"They're going to go to the hospital and talk to your father."

One of the police cars drove away.

"What about Bill?" It didn't seem right to leave him lying there.

"The firefighters will take care of him as soon as the fire burns itself out."

I heard the phone ringing and ran inside to pick it up. It was Flanna. She said they were wrapping my father's hand and putting a cast on Buzz's leg. She thought they would be back at the warehouse later that afternoon. I thanked her and went back outside.

Silver was gone.

* * *

I couldn't look when the firefighters zipped what remained of Bill's body into the black plastic bag and put it into the van. I'd known Bill Brewster my whole life. He and Doc had gone to school together, had worked as curators for the New York Zoological Society, and had been field partners all over the world. Now he was gone.

I watched as the police poked around the wreckage for a few minutes, then left without trying to ask me any more questions. The fire engine and van drove away right behind them.

I walked down to the water. There was nothing left of the boat except charred wood. The dock was gone as well.

Bill's death was going to be very hard on Doc. There was no one closer to my father than Bill Brewster. I had no idea what was going to happen to the expedition now that he was gone. And then there was Doc's and Buzz's injuries. The only way I could help Doc was to do whatever he wanted me to do. If this meant going back to the Home, going to summer school, or even to boarding school, I would do it. And I'd try to do it cheerfully, without complaint.

I pulled the back door wide open, so the bats could come home if they wanted to.

Flanna didn't drive up in the old truck until late that evening. Doc wore a sling, and his arm was wrapped in thick bandages. Buzz's leg was in a cast, and he had been given a pair of crutches to get around on. I helped Flanna get them inside. They immediately lay down on their cots without a word and went to sleep.

"They're on pain medication," Flanna said, tiredly. "Are you all right?"

"I guess," I said, but I wasn't sure. "Did the police figure out what happened?"

"They think it was an accident. Something to do with a fuel leak. We're lucky it didn't happen when we were on our way upriver."

Not lucky for Bill, I thought.

"I think I'll go to bed, too." Flanna said, wearily. "Good night, Jake."

"Good night."

CHAPTER 8

I was the first one awake the next morning. I got out of bed quietly and went outside, so I wouldn't disturb anyone. The bats still had not come back. I wandered around for about an hour, then went back inside to see if anyone was awake.

Doc was sitting on his bunk with a cup of coffee in his good hand. Buzz sat at the kitchen table with his cast resting on a chair. Flanna was making breakfast. The mood inside was very somber. I helped Flanna finish breakfast and brought plates over to Doc and Bill. Neither one of them was very hungry.

"I guess the big question is, what are we going to do now?" Doc said.

No one offered any answers.

Doc continued, "I'll take Bill's remains back to the States."

"So the expedition's off," Buzz said.

"Right," Doc said. "We don't have a boat and we don't have the money or the time to get another one. And with Bill gone, what's the point?"

No one had an answer for this, either.

There was a loud screeching noise out in the warehouse that startled all of us. Before I could get up to see what had caused it, there was a knock on the door. I opened it. It was Jay Silver. The screeching came from a large red-and-yellow macaw sitting on his shoulder. I let him and his bird in.

"Sorry," he said. "Scarlet doesn't like bats."

"Scarlet?"

"My macaw."

"But the bats are gone."

"They seem to have come back."

I stuck my head out the door. The bats were flying back into the warehouse.

I closed the door. "He's right."

Doc didn't look at all thrilled to see Silver.

"I just dropped by to see how you were doing," Silver said.

"Very thoughtful," Doc said, flatly.

"I don't believe I've had the pleasure, ma'am," Silver said. Scarlet almost lunged off his shoulder toward Flanna when he addressed her. "I'm afraid Scarlet isn't very fond of women."

"My name's Flanna Brenna. And you are?"

"Jay Silver."

"This is my son, Jake," Doc added.

"We met yesterday," I said.

Doc was surprised to hear this.

"I just wanted to make sure you were okay," Silver said. "And to tell you that I was sorry to hear about Bill."

There was an awkward silence and a lot of tension in the room, which I didn't understand.

"What will you do now?" Silver asked.

"We were just discussing that when you came in," Doc said.

"And?"

"We've decided to call the expedition off."

"I'm sorry to hear that," Silver said. "It's a shame after all the work you've put in."

"What's a shame," Doc said, "is that my best friend died twenty-four hours ago in a senseless accident. He and his dream were turned to ashes at the same exact moment."

"I know this is a difficult time for you, Dr. Lansa," Silver said, calmly. "But let me be frank. . . . I didn't know Bill well, but I can't imagine that he would want to see his dream abandoned like this."

"You didn't know him at all," Doc said. "What are you getting at, Silver?"

"I have a boat and it's still available."

"Forget it!"

Doc's hostility didn't seem to faze Silver.

Doc stared at the floor. After a long time he looked up at

Silver again. "I'm sorry, Silver. I don't mean to be so . . . Well . . ."

"I understand completely, Dr. Lansa."

"No you don't," Doc said. "You're the third skipper that's approached us since the boat blew up. At least you had the courtesy of waiting a day. The other two approached us while we were at the hospital. If my hand wasn't burned to a crisp, I would have slugged them."

"Who were they?" Silver asked.

"How would I know?" Doc said, irritably.

"It's not surprising, Dr. Lansa. You have an exploration permit to go upriver, and those are hard to come by."

"*Bill* had a permit! A lot of good it will do him now."

"The name on the permit could be changed," Silver said.

"I'd have to fly all the way to Brasília and see if I could get it transferred to me. This would take time. Too much time. And that's not the only problem.

"Buzz can't fly because of his leg. I can't fly with this bum hand. Without the ultralight, we would never be able to gather enough tracking data to prove that we can do this job. Not in the deadline that they've set for us.

"The other problem is the funding. We don't have enough money to hire you and your boat."

"I'm sure we can work something out," Silver said.

"That wouldn't solve the ultralight problem," Doc said.

"Perhaps your son could learn to fly the ultralight," Silver said.

My father laughed, which sort of hurt my feelings, but I understood why he laughed. It was a pretty wild suggestion.

"First of all, he's not a pilot. Second, he has to go back to the States in a couple of days and finish three years of high school. Third, I couldn't possibly put him in that kind of danger."

"Well," Silver said, "I'm just trying to come up with alternatives. My boat is fast. I think we can make up the time you'll lose getting the permit transferred. As far as your son becoming an ultralight pilot, that's your call. It's just an idea."

He opened the door and started to leave, then stopped and turned back.

"Still seems like a shame to give up after all the sacrifices that have been made." He continued through the door and closed it quietly behind him. Scarlet screeched again.

"Can you believe that guy?" Doc asked.

No one responded.

"Do you know him very well?" Flanna asked.

"Hardly at all. He was just one of the people who offered to take us upriver."

"Why didn't you let him?"

"There must have been a dozen skippers that offered their services. We turned all of them down. Bill and I decided that we would be better off getting our own boat." Doc shook his head. "Actually, we almost went with Silver. He was definitely a cut above most of the other skippers we talked to, but he was just too good to be true.

"We did some asking around about him. Silver's an ex-mercenary, soldier of fortune type, hired gun—whatever you want to call it—and we simply didn't trust him. He has other reasons for going upriver, but I have no idea what they are."

Flanna stirred her coffee slowly. "Still," she said, quietly, "Silver made some good points."

"About what?" Doc asked.

"About Bill and the jaguar preserve."

"Such as?"

"There have been a lot sacrifices made for this preserve. Bill was your best friend, you knew him better than any of us did. Do you think he would want you to give up?"

Doc rubbed the bandages on his arm. He didn't say anything for a long time.

"He wouldn't want that," Doc finally said. "But he would also know it was impossible to continue for the reasons I gave Silver."

Flanna looked at Buzz. "How dangerous are ultralights?"

Buzz grinned. "I think they're safer than driving around Manaus. Especially in our truck."

Doc frowned.

"How long would it take you to teach someone to fly the ultralight?" Flanna asked.

"Impossible!" Doc said. "You'll be too busy doing a botanical survey. That's part of Woolcott's conditions."

"How long?" Flanna persisted.

"A week," Buzz said. "Maybe a little longer. Depends on the student."

Flanna looked at me, then back at Doc. "I bet Jake would make an excellent ultralight pilot."

"No way," Doc sputtered.

"You told me he was a great pilot. You went on and on about it. Remember? You said that he was much more comfortable behind the controls than you were—"

"Yeah, but . . ."

"You and I could fly to Brasília today and meet with Woolcott. With his help we can probably get the expedition permit transferred. If Silver and Jake were ready, we could be on our way within a week."

I was thrilled that Doc had bragged about my flying, but I didn't say a word. In fact, I tried not to show any emotion, but at that moment I wanted to hug Flanna.

Doc looked at Buzz for help. "Jake has only flown by himself once in his life."

"To be honest with you, Doc, that's a big plus," Buzz replied. "One of the toughest things to do is teach a conventional pilot to fly an ultralight. The feel of the controls is totally different. I'd rather teach someone who has never flown. And besides, the helmet is almost a perfect fit. We'll have to do something about those foot pedals, though."

"You're not helping, Buzz," Doc said.

"I'm just telling it like it is."

"Jake doesn't even have a pilot's license."

"He doesn't need one to fly an ultralight. I'm sorry, Doc, but Flanna's right. If at all possible, Bill would want us to set up the preserve. And this is definitely a possibility. My busted strut will be healed up in a couple of months. Just in time to ride upriver with Woolcott and his team. I could take over for Jake then."

"Face it, Bob," Flanna said. "If you go back to the States and bury Bill without at least trying to fulfill his dream, you'll regret it for the rest of your life. Bill didn't want a tombstone. He wanted a jaguar preserve."

Doc looked at me. "I know I don't have to ask this, but are you game?"

He was right. He didn't have to ask.

Doc, Flanna, and I took the old truck down to the moorage to find Silver's boat and talk to him. His boat was called the *Tito*, and on the outside it looked as neat and well preserved as Silver was. As we walked up to the boat, we heard Scarlet scream. A second later, Silver came down from the wheelhouse with Scarlet perched on his shoulder.

"Welcome aboard." He didn't seem at all surprised to see us.

We climbed on board. Scarlet eyed Flanna suspiciously. Doc eyed Silver suspiciously.

"A change of mind, Dr. Lansa?"

"Maybe," Doc said. "If you have time, we'd like you to show us around."

"My pleasure."

The *Tito* was half again as big as the boat Doc and Bill had bought. The teak decks were bright with fresh varnish, and the brass fittings glittered in the morning sunlight. Silver took us below deck and showed us four roomy sleeping compartments.

"I'd recommend that you use these compartments for storage, not sleeping. Your equipment will be much safer down here."

"Where will we sleep?" Flanna asked.

"On deck. We'll put up mosquito netting. It's cooler up there, anyway."

He showed us the engine room, then took us up to the galley, which was good sized. It even had a large walk-in cooler. The last stop was the wheelhouse, or pilot house, where the boat was controlled. To get to it, we had to climb a steep metal stairway.

"As you can see," Silver explained, "I have pretty good equipment."

I pointed to the door opposite the bridge and asked him what it was.

"Those are my quarters."

I expected him to open the door and let us look inside, but apparently it wasn't part of the tour.

Doc and Flanna seemed impressed with the boat, and I know I was. I was also impressed with Silver. He was calm and competent. We went back down to the deck.

"How much would you charge to take us upriver?" Doc asked.

"How long do you need me?"

"I'm not exactly sure. Could be several months. Longer if things work out like we hope."

"I'll charge you a thousand bucks a month, and you pay for everything—provisions, fuel, boat repairs, and so on. And I want to be paid for three months up front, before we leave."

"I guess I don't understand," Doc said. "That's about a quarter of what the other skippers wanted, and their boats weren't half as nice as yours."

Silver shrugged his shoulders. "I have simple needs," he said.

"That doesn't really explain it, does it?"

"You're right," Silver admitted. "I want to go upriver, and I can't without an exploration permit. I wouldn't get a hundred miles before I got turned back."

"But why do you want to go upriver?"

"Like I told you before, Dr. Lansa. You're going to an area of the Amazon I've never been to before. I just want to take a look around. I'm not a conservationist like you are. I'm just curious. I'll let you talk about it privately." He climbed back up to the wheelhouse.

"I told you he was too good to be true," Doc said.

"I agree," Flanna said. "But if he gets us to the preserve safely, what difference does it make?"

Doc looked around the deck as he thought about it. "I guess if we can get the permit, and if Jake can learn to fly the Morpho, we'll give it a go. But those are a lot of ifs."

CHAPTER 9

D oc and Flanna got tickets to leave for Brasília that afternoon. Doc also arranged to have Bill's remains flown back to his family in the States. Silver offered to drive them to the airport in his Landrover, which was a lot nicer than our truck.

Doc's final words to Buzz were: "By the time I get back, if I'm not convinced that Jake can fly that contraption of yours safely, then the deal's off."

"Yes, sir!" Buzz saluted, and almost fell over because of the crutches.

Doc shook his head in despair. We watched them drive away, then Buzz turned to me. "We don't have much time to accomplish this mission." I followed him back into the warehouse. "I'm afraid I'm not going to be much help with this bum leg, Jake. Go ahead and take the tarp off and pull the Morpho outside."

I managed to get it through the door without ripping a wing off.

"Are you ready?"

I looked at the Morpho, not sure if I would ever be ready and hopeful that I wouldn't let Buzz down by flying it into the ground. "I guess so," I said, and ran back in and got the helmet. When I got back outside, I slipped it on my head.

Buzz looked at me quizzically for a few moments. "I don't think you'll need that. Unless you have a tendency to bump your head a lot."

"I don't think I should fly without a helmet."

"I don't think you should, either. But you're not even close to flying yet. Bring the big toolbox out here."

I ran back inside and lugged the toolbox back out. I figured he had a few adjustments to make before I took off. I was badly mistaken.

"The first thing you're going to do is to take this thing apart," Buzz said. "Every wire, nut, bolt, and cotter pin. Then you're going to put it all back together again, and I want it to look just like it does now."

I thought he was joking. It would take hours to get it apart, and I wasn't sure if I could ever put it back together again.

"I'm not a mechanic," I said.

"And you won't be a mechanic when you finish, either. But you'll understand how the Morpho works. And if something shakes loose in the wild blue, you'll know what it is and whether it's going to make you fall out of the sky. I'll tell you the names of the things as you take them apart. Then you'll tell me the names when you put them back together. We'll make a game out of it. I hope for your sake that you're better with tools than your old man. Get ready to have your mind bent."

Not only did my mind get bent, but my knuckles got bruised and my eyes blurred over with sweat from the stifling heat.

It took me hours to get the ultralight apart. And Buzz was the reason. Every time I unhooked or unscrewed something, he'd ask what it was and what it did. If I didn't know, I'd guess. If I was wrong, which I often was, he'd tell me the proper name and function. Periodically he'd point at something with his crutch from the growing pile of nuts, bolts, and tubing, and ask me what it was. If I didn't answer correctly, he'd make me reassemble the connecting pieces until I could tell him exactly what it was and what it did.

"Were you in the army?" I asked.

"Fat chance. They said I was too thin. Guess I wasn't a big enough target."

"I think you missed your calling as a drill sergeant."

I don't know how long it took. When the sun went down, I thought Buzz would call it a day. But no, he had me run an extension cord and hook up a light, so I could continue.

Silver dropped by a couple of times and watched for a while. He said that he had a crew coming in the next day to rebuild the dock. As soon as it was finished, he planned to move his boat down from the moorage.

Finally I pulled out the last cotter pin and unscrewed the

last nut. My hands were swollen, I was hungry, and I couldn't remember being more exhausted. Buzz nodded, turned off the light, and hobbled back into the bunk room.

All I wanted to do was get something to eat and climb into bed, but Buzz had other ideas. We began ultralight ground school. The first lecture was on weather flying. Buzz went on for over two hours. The bottom line was not to take off in the Morpho unless the weather was perfect and looked as if it would stay perfect throughout the flight.

When he was finished with the lecture, I stumbled into the bathroom. When I got out, Buzz was in his bunk sound asleep, snoring away. I grabbed some food, collapsed on my own bunk, and almost dozed off in midchew.

A few hours later, I felt something hard poking me in the back. It was Buzz's crutch. He was a cruel man.

"Rise and shine, Ace!"

It took me all that day and half the night to get the ultralight back together again. Every time I made a mistake, Buzz made me back up a few steps and start again. A couple of times I got so mad at him that I had to walk to the dock to calm down. That didn't seem to offend Buzz in the least. Silver and his hired help were making much better progress on the dock than I was on the ultralight. I envied them because they got to work in the water, where it was relatively cool.

When I finally got the Morpho back together, I held up the last cotter pin and ceremoniously snapped it through the end of the last bolt.

Buzz looked at his watch. "That didn't take you as long as I thought it would."

I wasn't sure if he meant that as a compliment or not.

"So you understand how it works now?"

"Yes," I said, weakly.

"Do you think you could repeat the assembly?"

"I think so," I said, praying he wouldn't ask me to do it again.

"I think you can, too. Let's go in and get some sleep."

The phone was ringing when we got inside. Buzz picked it up. It was Doc.

"I've never seen anything like it," Buzz said into the phone. "Jake's a natural born pilot. It's incredible!" He winked at me and held his finger to his lips. "That's great! When do you think you'll be back? . . . Silver finished the dock today. He'll bring his boat over tomorrow. . . . He seems okay to me. I don't think you'll have any problems with him. . . . Okay. Bye." He hung up the phone.

"Flanna and Doc met with Woolcott today. He was very sorry to hear about Bill and he thinks they should continue with the expedition. He's going to help them get the permit transferred."

"What were you saying about Silver?" I asked.

"Doc just wanted to know what I thought of him. He's just being cautious."

"What was that stuff about my being a 'natural born pilot'? I haven't even flown the Morpho yet."

"Just wanted to bolster his spirits a bit. He was very pleased."

* * *

The next morning I was up before the crutch poked me. Today was the day I'd be flying, or so I thought. I made a pot of coffee for Buzz, then went outside to look at the Morpho. I sure hoped I had put it together right.

About half an hour later, Buzz joined me outside. "You have one more little chore before you climb into the cockpit."

I frowned.

"You need to learn how to pack the Morpho's parachute."

I didn't even know it had a parachute.

Buzz hobbled back inside and pointed at one of the boxes. I opened it and pulled something out that looked like a backpack. He told me to haul it outside and pull the chute out of the pack. There were actually two parachutes in the pack, a primary chute and a smaller, backup chute in case the first one malfunctioned.

"This is a ballistic parachute," he said. "There's an explosive charge in the pack. When you pull the string, it shoots the parachute out away from the ultralight so it doesn't get tangled up in the wings."

"You mean you don't bail out?"

"Nope. If you get in trouble, you pull the cord and you and the Morpho float to the ground like a dry autumn leaf. Ideally."

"Have you ever had to use a parachute?"

"One time," he said. "And I got hung up in an oak tree and nearly broke my neck."

This was not encouraging. "The rain forest is nothing but trees," I pointed out.

"I know," he said. "You probably won't need the chute. And if you do, you'll have to be very careful."

Great!

Buzz had me pack and repack the chute until I could have done it with blindfolds on.

"I think you have that down," he finally said. "*Now* you can put the helmet on."

I spent most of the day doing "touch-and-goes." This exercise consisted of flying the Morpho down the flat area in back of the warehouse, never getting more than about ten feet off the ground.

"The idea is to get used to the throttle and other controls," he said. "I want you to be able to land with your eyes closed."

The ultralight's engine was very loud despite the advanced muffler system Buzz had put on it. And at only ten feet off the ground, the Morpho was very difficult to control. I felt that I was going to crash at any moment. By late afternoon, Buzz was satisfied that I could take the ultralight off and land it. Every muscle in my body ached, and I didn't know if this was from being jarred every time I landed or if the soreness was caused by tension.

"I think you've had enough for today," he said.

"Tomorrow we'll put the pontoons on and see how you do with water landings."

"You know, Buzz, Doc's going to be back here in a few days and expects me to know how to fly this thing."

Buzz laughed. "Believe it or not, you've already learned the hardest part—getting the ultralight up and getting it back down safely. The actual flying part is easy."

Silver and his men finished the dock that evening, and he said that he would bring the *Tito* over the next day.

Early the following morning Buzz told me how to attach the pontoons to the Morpho's landing gear.

Landing and taking off from the water was much harder than landing and taking off from land. The water caused a lot more drag on the ultralight, and I had to get more speed before I could take off. When I landed, I had to watch out for the current and the crosswind so I wouldn't flip the Morpho over. I found that if one float started to come up off the water, I had to lean my weight toward it to get it back down on the surface. After twenty touch-and-goes, I was drenched. I taxied over to the dock where Buzz was standing and shut the engine down.

He looked up at the sky. "I guess it's time to hit the wild blue yonder. But first you've got to change into some dry clothes. At two thousand feet it can get darn cold when you're wet."

"Two thousand feet?"

He nodded. "Thereabouts," he said. "I want you to do

some lazy circles. Just keep the warehouse in sight, and I'll keep in touch with this handheld radio."

After I changed my clothes I topped the fuel tank off with gas, buckled myself into the seat, and flipped the visor down on my helmet.

"Okay," he said over the radio. "Let her rip."

I took a deep breath and started the engine. When the oil pressure was right, I pulled the throttle all the way out. In seconds I was airborne, but instead of reducing power and landing again, I pulled the control stick toward me and I was off. At first I was very nervous, but this feeling was soon replaced with exhilaration. I was actually flying the Morpho, and it was awesome.

"What's your altitude?" Buzz said.

I looked at the altimeter. "About a thousand feet."

"Good. Bring her around counterclockwise, keeping the same pitch, then level out at two thousand feet. You're doing great."

I could see for miles, although the view was obscured somewhat by a thick haze of smoke from all the wood burning. In the distance, miles from the river, I saw the leading edge of the rain forest.

I took the ultralight up to two thousand feet and leveled it off. Buzz was a little speck standing near the dock. I was going fifty knots. At that speed, the controls were very responsive. To turn left, all it took was a little pressure on the stick and rudder pedal.

I felt every puff of wind and the different temperatures as I flew through the thermals. Buzz had me fly half a dozen wide loops around the warehouse, then told me to come in for a landing before I forgot how to get down. The landing was a little rough, but I got down safely and taxied over to the dock.

"Not bad," Buzz said. "Not bad at all."

"It was wonderful!"

He smiled. "Let's check this machine over, refuel, and then you can get back up there again."

At the end of the day, after we put the ultralight into the warehouse, I was still flying even though I was on the ground. Buzz was very pleased with how I had done.

CHAPTER 10

I spent the next day practicing different maneuvers in the Morpho with Buzz watching. That evening he and Silver drove off in the Landrover on what Buzz called a "secret mission." They didn't get back until late.

The next morning Buzz announced that we were going to play hide-and-seek.

"What do you mean?"

"Simple," he explained. "Last night we scattered half a dozen radio collars around the countryside. You're going to find them with your receiver and the global positioning system. When you get the collar's position, radio it in to me and I'll verify it and give you the frequency of the next collar."

I took off. When I got to two thousand feet, I leveled out and entered the number of the first collar on my receiver. As I flew in slow, wide circles, I listened carefully for the collar's signal. Halfway through the loop I heard a very faint

beep . . . beep . . . beep as the antennas picked up the signal.
All I had to do now was to follow the beeping until I thought
I was over the top of it. I had radio-tracked from an airplane
when I was in Kenya, but I hadn't been flying the airplane at
the same time. Doing both wasn't easy. I managed to lose
the signal twice before I figured out which direction it was
coming from. The beeping got louder the closer I got to the
collar. Then it began to fade, and I knew I had passed over
the top of it. I swung the ultralight around. When I thought
the signal was loudest, I punched the button on the GPS and
radioed the longitude and latitude to Buzz.

"Close enough," he said, and gave me the frequency of
the next collar.

It took me the rest of the day to find the remaining collars.
I had to fly back to the warehouse five times and refuel.

That evening Silver offered to collect the collars and hide
them by himself. Buzz gratefully accepted. His leg had been
bothering him all day from bouncing around in the
Landrover the night before.

Buzz and I hit our bunks pretty early, but for some reason I couldn't fall asleep. I hadn't sent a dispatch to the
Home since I learned that I might be staying down here. I
kept putting it off because I didn't know what to say. Taw
would be sorry to hear about Bill and disappointed that I
wasn't coming back in a few days.

I lay in the dark for a long time thinking about Doc,
Flanna, the expedition, and flying. I was excited about going

with them, but I wished that Doc had wanted me to go instead of being forced into it by Bill's death. Why didn't he get in touch with me while I was at the Home? Why didn't he tell me about Flanna? A little voice went off in my head—*for the same reason you don't want to tell Taw you're not coming back home.* I realized that it was difficult to tell people things that they don't want to hear. Maybe this was the reason Doc hadn't contacted me.

I got up and slipped outside, thinking that a short walk might help me sleep. There was a light coming from the *Tito*'s wheelhouse. I wandered over to see what Silver was up to. I stepped aboard and called out his name, but he didn't answer.

I climbed the steep stairs to the wheelhouse. He wasn't there, nor was Scarlet, but the door to his cabin was slightly ajar. I knocked and called his name again. Nothing. I opened the door the rest of the way.

"Silver?"

The only light in his cabin came from a small lamp on the desk. I stepped inside. His cabin was twice the size of the cabins below deck. There was a simple bed, an oak desk, and a large map table. Along one wall were floor-to-ceiling shelves overflowing with books. I was happy to see them and I hoped he would let me borrow a few for the long trip up the Amazon. He had some of the same books about explorers I had read back at the Home. He also had books on history, animals, and several works on the indigenous people of the Amazon. Some of the volumes looked very old, with tattered leather covers. I pulled one out and looked at the yellowed pages. It was written in Portuguese.

I was going to pull another book off the shelf when it occurred to me that Silver might not want me snooping around in his private quarters. I decided I better get out of there, but as I was turning to leave, the framed photographs above Silver's desk caught my attention. I went over for a closer look. A much younger version of Silver looked out from the photos. He had dark, close-cropped hair and was wearing military fatigues. The photos must have been taken during the Vietnam War. There were other soldiers in the photos with Silver—probably buddies of his in the same platoon. Below these photos were several color snapshots of Silver playing with a young Indian boy. The boy was about two years old. Silver was smiling in every shot and seemed to be really happy.

I heard a noise behind me. Before I could turn around, someone shoved me into the bookshelves, then grabbed me and slammed me down on the floor. I caught a glimpse of his face in the dim light. He had a small scar on the left side of his face. That's the last thing I remember before I blacked out.

* * *

I don't know how long I was out, but when I came to, I was still on the floor and Silver was kneeling next to me. I had a splitting headache and my vision was fuzzy.

I started to sit up, but Silver gently pushed me back

down. "You better stay where you are for a minute."

"What happened?"

"Looks like we had a little break-in. How many were there?"

"Just one, I think."

"Did you happen to see what he looked like?"

"Not really. It was pretty dark. I think he had a scar on his face."

Silver nodded. "Can you sit up? Real slow." He helped me into a sitting position. The room spun around, and it was all I could do not to throw up. "You must have disturbed his little party."

I looked around the room. It was a mess. The mattress on Silver's bed had been shredded. Every book was pulled off the shelf; all the drawers had been opened and dumped on the floor.

I took a deep breath. "I didn't disturb his party," I admitted. "He disturbed mine." I explained what I had been doing in his cabin and apologized for going in there without asking.

Silver didn't seem upset about it.

"Did he take anything?" I asked.

"Nothing important. Do you think you can stand?"

He helped me to my feet and assisted me out into the wheelhouse, where the light was better.

"That's quite a bump," he said, looking at the back of my head.

"I'll be all right. Do you need some help cleaning up?"

"No, I'll take care of it. You need to get some rest."

He walked with me to the warehouse, stopping outside the door. "Can you make it from here?"

"Sure."

"One more thing," Silver said. "Why don't we keep this between you and me? No use upsetting Buzz and your father. They have enough to worry about as it is."

He was right. The incident would just confirm Doc's belief that it was too dangerous for me down here. I told him that I wouldn't tell anyone and apologized again for going into his cabin.

"No harm done. Well, except for your head."

* * *

Buzz woke me with a poke from his crutch. "We have work to do, Ace."

I'd only slept about four hours, and my head felt as if it were going to burst. I didn't really feel like flying, but I knew I had to. I stumbled into the bathroom and took a long shower. The bump on the back of my head was very tender. I walked back to the bunk room. Buzz had managed to cook breakfast, despite his crutches. He was obviously feeling better than he had the day before. I sat down at the table and started eating. Buzz was standing behind me drinking a cup of coffee.

"What happened to your head?" he asked in alarm.

"I went out for a walk last night and bumped it on something."

"That's more than a bump. Are you going to be okay?"

"I'll be fine." Eventually, I thought.

"Our friend Silver told me he did a great job hiding those collars last night. It's not going to be as easy today," he warned.

Nothing was going to be easy today. I finished breakfast and climbed into the Morpho.

Buzz was right: finding the collars wasn't easy. It took more than three hours to find the first two. As I was flying around trying to pick up the signal from the third collar, a call came over the radio.

"Morpho, this is base," Buzz said. "Please return immediately. Over."

"What's up? Over."

"Just get back here," Buzz said. "And you better make the best landing of your life. Over and out."

I wondered what was going on. I turned the Morpho around and headed back. From a distance I saw four people standing on the dock, but it wasn't until I got closer that I recognized them—Buzz, Silver, Flanna, and my father. I hadn't expected Doc and Flanna back so soon. I wondered if it meant they hadn't gotten the expedition permit.

I flew over them and waggled my wings. They waved back. Buzz was right: I needed to make a perfect landing; otherwise Doc might call the whole expedition off. I only wished that my head felt better.

I followed the river downwind and banked the Morpho

to the left for my final approach. I eased the power off and gently pulled the nose back until the Morpho began to stall. The Morpho shuttered slightly. A second later, the pontoons skimmed the surface of the water with hardly a skip. I breathed a deep sigh of relief.

"Not bad, Ace," Buzz said over the radio.

I taxied over to the dock. Silver grabbed the wing and held the ultralight steady while I unbuckled the belt and got out.

"That was pretty good," Doc said. "I really didn't think you'd be able to pick it up that quickly."

"He had a great instructor," Buzz said humbly.

"Did you get the permit?" I asked.

"We did. Looks like you'll be tracking jaguars in a few weeks."

* * *

It took all of the next day to get the supplies loaded on the boat. I spent that time dismantling the Morpho, so we could get it on board. When Doc saw me taking it apart, he threw a minor fit because he thought there would be no one to put it back together once we got there. Buzz assured him that his son had *not* inherited his lack of mechanical ability. Doc calmed down about it, but he was still skeptical.

That evening I sent a fax to the Home:

> *Dear Taw,*
> *There's been a terrible accident down here. Doc and*

Bill's boat exploded in Manaus and Bill was killed. Doc's hand and arm were burned in the fire, but he'll be fine. The expedition's pilot, Buzz Lindbergh, broke his leg when the boat blew up. They've asked me to fly the airplane they're using to track the jaguars—at least for the time being. So it looks like I won't be coming back to Poughkeepsie for a while.

We're leaving tomorrow for the preserve. Unfortunately, I won't be able to send any more dispatches for the time being because I'll be on a boat going up the Amazon River.

I'll miss you! When I get back, we'll take that trip to Arizona you were talking about.

Please give my love to all the other "inmates" and tell them that when I get back, we'll have a Press Conference they'll never forget.

All my love, Jake

P.S. Tell Peter to go for walks with you every day. You need to be in good shape for our trip to Arizona!

The next morning Doc and Buzz looked at a map and picked a tentative base camp.

"I'll bring Woolcott up there in a couple of months," Buzz said. He turned to me. "And Jake, you better take good care of my baby."

I told him I would.

Just as the sun was coming up, we said good-bye to Buzz and started the long journey up the Amazon River.

The River

CHAPTER 11

As soon as we were under way, Silver came down from the wheelhouse and laid down some rules. The first was that we were to keep a loaded shotgun nearby at all times. Flanna didn't like this idea at all, and Doc wasn't far behind her. He had never been fond of guns.

"Guns are nothing but trouble," Flanna said.

"The shotgun is to stop trouble, not start it," Silver said.

"Don't you think you're being a little paranoid?" Doc asked.

Silver was clearly irritated by their reaction. He leaned on the rail and looked across to the far shore as if he was thinking of an appropriate response.

"While you're down here telling us to arm ourselves like we're in the middle of a war zone," Flanna said, "who's steering the boat? We won't need the shotgun if we sink."

Silver turned and looked at her. "The boat is on automatic pilot," he said calmly.

"And does the automatic pilot tell you when a floating log is going to ram the boat?" Flanna asked.

"No," Silver said. "Scarlet does that for me. Her eyesight is much better than mine. And yours, I might add. She'll let me know if something's coming along."

"Oh, that's great," Doc said in disgust. "You want us to carry shotguns, and we have a macaw for a first mate."

"Okay, Doc," Silver said quietly. "I guess it's time we got down to it. And I'm glad it's happening now rather than further upriver, where we might not have time for this type of discussion.

"As you know, we're going into uncharted territory. Outside of the fact that it will be hot, and filled with nasty insects, poisonous snakes, and debilitating diseases, I don't know what to expect."

"I've been upriver before," Doc reminded him.

"That was a long time ago, Dr. Lansa. Things have changed a great deal. The interior has been opened up and it's filled with men who will murder you for a hundred dollars, or for pleasure, if the mood strikes them. There's virtually no law enforcement, and what little there is, is so corrupt that it would be better to have no law at all. It's worse than the Wild West ever was."

My father thought about this for a few moments. "If it's as bad as you say, why didn't you have us hire a crew to protect us?"

"Because that's the worst thing we could possibly do!"

Silver said. "The reason most expeditions fail is because they take too many people. More mouths to feed, more personality conflicts, more disagreements about what to do when things go bad. Once the preserve is set up, you can bring in as many people as you want. But for now there's a world of difference between four people and half a dozen people. Believe me, I know! I've done this before. Which brings me to the most important point of this conversation and perhaps the foundation of your and Dr. Brenna's little problem."

"And what's that?"

"I'm the captain of this boat. Period! I'm in charge of getting us to the preserve, and you're in charge of getting the preserve going."

Scarlet let out an ear-piercing scream.

"Excuse me," Silver said, and climbed up to the wheel-house.

"He's crazy," Doc said. "And I must have been crazy to think this was going to work."

The boat lurched to the right. A few seconds later, we passed a very large tree floating just below the surface of the water. None of us would have seen it until after it had put a hole in the boat the size of a washing machine. I looked at Flanna and Doc.

"How did Silver time that?" Flanna asked, clearly impressed with Scarlet's seamanship.

"You were with him for a week, Jake," Doc said. "Do you trust him?"

I thought about Silver helping me on the day of the explosion and after the break-in. Other than this I had had very little contact with him. He kept to himself most of the time. "I don't know," I said. "I guess he's trustworthy."

Silver climbed back down to the deck. "Where were we?"

Doc shook his head. "I'll admit that I haven't been upriver in a while, but I still don't like the shotgun idea."

"I'm not asking you to shoot anybody," Silver said. "I just want you to keep the shotgun close by, to discourage those who might want to shoot you."

Doc looked at Flanna. She nodded. "All right, Silver," he said. "You're the captain."

"Good. It will take us three weeks to get to the site if everything goes well, but things rarely go well in this country." He climbed back up to the wheelhouse.

* * *

The days on the river were long, hot, and pretty boring. It rained nearly every day. Dark clouds swooped in, dumping inches of rain, then disappeared as quickly as they had come.

Doc was not in the best mood. His hand and arm were not healing properly, and I think he was in constant pain. And this wasn't his only problem. Bill's death was eating away at him. The way he usually dealt with tragedy was to throw himself into a frenzy of work.

The first few days on the river he was able to keep the

demons of grief away by staying busy. He set up our living quarters on deck by hanging the hammocks and mosquito netting. He did an inventory of all our supplies and calculated how long they would last us. After this, he worked on the telemetry gear we would use to track jaguars. He rebuilt receivers, cataloged collar frequencies, and set up a tracking database on his laptop computer. But then there was nothing else for him to do. He spent a good portion of the day in his hammock watching the shore go by, which had changed a great deal since his last trip.

Doc was horrified by the amount of rain forest destruction we saw on the way upriver. Twenty years ago, he and Bill had spent six weeks along the Amazon as graduate students. Many of the lush green places they had visited were gone now—replaced by mining, timber, and oil operations. Silver didn't say anything, but I could see that he was as appalled by the destruction as we were. Every once in a while I would catch him staring at the devastated landscape and shaking his head in quiet dismay.

"The search for gold is the worst," Flanna told me. "Even a vague rumor of gold brings thousands of people into the rain forest. They knock the trees down, burn the vegetation, cut roads, build crude shantytowns, and kill every animal they can find for food and to sell their skins. When they abandon an area, there's nothing left but an ugly scar that won't heal for a hundred years, if at all."

She went on to explain how they find the gold.

"Prospectors follow a small tributary up to the head-waters, then pan their way downstream until they find gold. They then work their way back up until they find the source of the gold by digging alongshore. When they find the source, they follow it to the rock formation and dig around the formation until they find the vein.

"But that's not the worst of it. The trees are cut, the rivers polluted, and the Indians who have the misfortune of living near the mining camps are either killed or turned into slave laborers."

"This doesn't sound much different from what happened to the Indians in North America," I said.

"It's exactly the same," Silver agreed. "And it will probably never change."

As we got further away from Manaus, I thought we would start seeing animals along the river, but about the only animals we saw were vultures roosting in the trees near the shantytowns.

Every few days we made a brief stop at a fuel barge to fill the *Tito*'s gas tanks. Silver said that when we got further upriver, fuel would be harder to find and much more expensive.

There were a lot of other boats on the river besides ours—barges with ramshackle houses built on them like floating villages; small fishing boats; large supply boats; ferries carrying travelers; floating brothels that moved prostitutes from one town to the next; and produce boats

that carried fruits, vegetables, meat, and fresh eggs from
their onboard chicken coops.

There were also patrol boats, which stopped us several
times to check our passports and make certain that our
expedition permit was in order. Sometimes the patrols
were stationed at a fuel barge, and they checked us out
when we came in to fill up. Other times they made us stop
in midriver, much to Silver's irritation. We would have to
head toward shore and throw the anchors out. The officers
came aboard and looked through everything we had under
Silver's ever-watchful eye.

Flanna said they had started the permit system to stop
foreigners from plundering the rain forest without giving
anything back to the country. Silver's opinion was that government officials used the permits as a way of making sure
they got a cut of the action before people left town with the
goods.

During the day, Silver kept the boat moving up the middle
of the river. Doc offered to take over the helm so Silver could
rest, but Silver told him that he and Scarlet had everything
under control. Toward evening he would find a good spot
about thirty feet from shore and throw out the anchors. We
stayed away from shore to keep the insects from eating us alive.

When we anchored for the evening, we'd go for a swim,
then Flanna and Doc would slather themselves with insect
repellent and take Silver's inflatable Zodiac to shore to look
around. Silver didn't like the idea, but they reached a

compromise by agreeing to take the shotgun with them. I went with them a couple of times, but stopped when it dawned on me that they might want to be alone with each other. They always left the shotgun in the Zodiac, but I didn't tell Silver this.

I was beginning to really like Flanna, despite my misgivings about her and Doc's romance—if you could call it that. Doc hadn't been in what I would call a romantic mood since Bill's death. I could see at times that his attitude hurt Flanna's feelings, but she didn't push the issue and gave him plenty of space. She was smart enough to know that this was the only way to handle my father. She changed Doc's bandages twice a day, ignoring his complaints while she smeared her special salve on his tender skin. She was friendly to me without being overly friendly, which I appreciated. I guess she knew how to handle me as well.

She told me she had been born in Ireland but raised in Oregon. Her interest in botany came from her parents, who owned a large plant nursery outside Portland. They wanted her to become a botanist and take over the nursery one day. She wanted to become a doctor and travel.

"I split the difference with them," she said. "I became a botanist, but I specialize in medicinal rain forest plants."

"Where did you learn to climb?"

"We had giant oak trees on our property. When I was a kid, I spent more time in them than I did on the ground. When the trees got too manageable for me, I took up rock climbing, learned to use ropes, and adapted the techniques for canopy exploration."

Most evenings our first mate, Scarlet, would leave her perch in the wheelhouse and spend the night in the forest. "Shore leave," Silver called it. He didn't know where she went or what she did on these nocturnal flights. And he didn't care, as long as she was back before sunrise. "And sober," he added.

He and Scarlet had been mates for ten years. He bought her from an Indian when she was no bigger than the palm of his hand. "'Ugliest chick you've ever seen," he said. "I didn't even know what kind of parrot she was until she grew up. I hand-fed her every two hours for weeks."

Silver stayed pretty much to himself. He spent his days in the wheelhouse and his nights in his cabin. We hadn't had any conflicts since the first day out, but there was always some underlying tension in the air. He was different from what he had been onshore—kind of edgy and somewhat nervous. A couple of times, late at night, I heard him leave the wheel-house and come down to the deck. I watched him through the mosquito netting as I lay in my hammock. With his shotgun cradled in his arms, he would take about ten steps, then stop and stand perfectly still as if listening for something. I had no idea what he was up to. The only sounds were the steady hum of insects and the water lapping against the boat.

One evening, after Flanna and Doc had rowed to shore, I went up to the wheelhouse to talk with Silver. I found him

Jaguar

in his cabin sitting at his map table, staring at a chart. I started the conversation by asking him about Colonel Fawcett and his search for the lost Muribeca mines.

"Colonel Fawcett was a courageous man and a great explorer," Silver said. "But he was chasing after something that never existed. The fruitless search killed him, his son, and his son's friend. It's a tragedy that's as old as the rain forest."

What I really wanted to talk to him about were the snapshots of him and the young Indian boy. In these photos Silver looked happy and relaxed, as if he were at peace with himself and the world. It was a very different portrait from the tense and suspicious Silver that I had come to know. I walked over to the desk where the photos were hanging.

"What else can I do for you, Jake?" Silver asked.

"I was wondering about these photographs. You were in Vietnam?"

"Three tours of duty. Special Forces."

"And these other photographs of you with the young boy?"

"That was a long time ago," he said, with a faraway look in his eyes. "That boy is my son, Tito."

"Like your boat."

He nodded. "His mother—my wife—was Alicia. She was a Huaorani woman from Ecuador and we lived together along the Rio Curaray."

"What happened?"

"I'm not sure," he said. "I had to go away on a job. I was

118

away for three months. When I got back, they were gone. That was ten years ago. Alicia's family might have come by and convinced her to live with them elsewhere. They weren't very fond of me—not that most native people have any reason to love whites. Or maybe she joined a different group of Indians and disappeared into the forest with them. She missed her people," he paused for a moment. "Tito would be a little younger than you now."

"Did you look for them?"

"For a very long time, but I never found them. It's like they disappeared from the face of the earth. I still ask around, of course. And I named my boat after Tito, thinking that one day a young man would come up to me and tell me that his name is the same."

I wondered if this was his real reason for traveling upriver.

"That's when I got Scarlet. I was bringing her back as a gift for little Tito."

He looked back at his chart. I waited around for a few moments, hoping he would tell me more, but he didn't. I left him alone.

CHAPTER 12

The days and nights flowed into each other, and I lost track of how long we had been on the river. One afternoon, earlier than usual, Silver steered the boat toward shore and let the anchors down.

"What's the problem?" Doc asked.

"I don't know," Silver said. "But we're losing oil pressure." He went below to the engine room and came back up a couple of hours later covered in grease and sweat. "We'll have to pull in somewhere and find a mechanic."

* * *

The next morning Silver brought the *Tito* into a good-sized moorage near a mining settlement. Silver grabbed his shotgun and jumped down to the dock.

"Don't leave the boat," he said. "There's nothing but trouble here."

I watched him as he strode purposefully along the dock. Everyone he encountered along the way made room for him to pass. When he got to the end of the dock, he took a well-beaten path cut into a steep bank, which I assumed led to the town.

Along the bank were several small shacks with rusty tin roofs. Laundry flapped in the wind. Gangs of children wearing nothing but ragged T-shirts played in the black mud alongshore and threw sticks and rocks at any mangy dog that was fool enough to get within range. The air was foul. It smelled like rotting meat and fruit mixed with oil and urine.

I wasn't tempted to leave the boat, nor were Flanna and Doc. They dozed in their hammocks. I wondered how anyone could live in a place like this.

After about an hour of staring at the sad scenery, I got kind of bored and found the binoculars. I wanted to see if I could spot Silver coming down the jungle path before he got to the dock.

I focused the lenses on the hillside, looking for a likely opening in the thick growth, when I saw a man watching *us* through binoculars! As soon as he saw me, he took the binoculars away from his face and I saw the scar. I could have sworn it was the same man who had broken into Silver's cabin.

I almost shouted out to Doc and Flanna, but caught myself. They didn't know anything about the break-in. It was Silver's and my little secret. If Doc found out about it at this late date, he would be very upset with both me and Silver. The expedition didn't need this kind of problem.

Jaguar

The man started up the path in the same direction Silver had gone. I needed to warn Silver that the man was here. I looked back at Doc and Flanna—both of them were sound asleep. I jumped to the dock and ran.

The path was steep and muddy. I was out of breath when I got to the top. No sign of the man. I continued on, and half a mile later I got to the town. Nothing could have prepared me for what I saw. There were hundreds of men standing and trudging through deep, smelly mud. Most of them carried guns or machetes. There were no real streets—just dozens of shacks with narrow spaces between them. Silver was wrong: it wasn't like the Wild West; it was like another planet.

I'd never be able to find Silver in a place like this. I couldn't even ask anyone, because I didn't speak Portuguese. My best bet was to wait for Silver and catch him on his way down. I looked one more time at the men milling and standing around, wondering why they stayed in this miserable place. That's when I saw the man again. At least I thought it was the same man. He was walking up a narrow trail that ran along the hill behind the town. I'd never catch him before he reached the top, but I might be able to get an idea of where he was going. I jogged over to the trail and started up.

A constant string of exhausted-looking men passed me on their way down the path. They were completely covered with dried mud. What were they doing up there? I wondered. When I got to the top, I found out.

Jaguar

The trail came to an end near the edge of a giant pit. The hole was five times the size of a football field and at least three hundred feet deep. Hundreds of men swung picks and shoveled rocks from patches of ground measuring about ten feet square. The rocks were put into large burlap bags. The men without shovels or picks hefted the bags to their shoulders, then waited in line to climb up a series of rickety ladders leading to the top of the pit. When they reached the top, they dumped their bags into wooden sluice boxes, then climbed back down into the pit and started all over again.

They were mining for gold, and each tiny patch of ground was a claim. The men carrying rocks were probably laborers, working for pennies a day. As I watched, a man on a ladder lost his load. This started a chain reaction, and half a dozen men fell several feet to the rocky ground. The work didn't stop; in fact, it barely paused. The ladder was straightened, and within seconds it was filled with men carrying bags that weighed more than they did.

It was the most depressing thing I had ever seen. I didn't care anymore whether I found the man with the scar. I just wanted to get back to the boat. I hoped Silver would return soon so we could leave.

As I walked back through town, I saw a group of men standing in a circle around an Indian, shouting and laughing at him. One of the men punched the Indian in the face, and he fell to the ground. When I saw this, something snapped inside me. It was almost as if the man had punched me instead of the Indian.

"Leave him alone!" I shouted. I broke through the circle and faced the man who had slugged the Indian. He looked at me and laughed. I hit him in the stomach as hard as I could. The man was stunned, but not from the punch. I tried to help the Indian off the ground, but someone pulled me away from him. The man I hit shouted at me in Portuguese, then slapped me. I tried to get away, but the man who held me was too strong. The man slapped me again. He was about to slap me a third time, when a loud explosion erupted—his hand stopped in midswing.

It was Silver. He pumped another shell into the shotgun, leveled the barrel at the man's chest, and said something to him. The man said something back. Silver tightened his finger on the trigger. The man held up both hands and said something else. He turned to me and smiled, then ruffled my hair, as if the whole thing were a big joke. Silver didn't smile. The man holding me loosened his grip.

"They were beating up the Indian," I said. I looked for the Indian, but he had slipped away.

"They've been known to do that," Silver said. He didn't take the gun off the man. "I thought I told you to stay on the boat."

"I know, but I saw—"

"What's going on, Jake?" It was Doc, out of breath from running up the path.

"What are you doing here?" Silver asked him.

"I woke up and Jake was gone, so I went to look for him."

"And who's guarding the boat?"

124

"Flanna's down there."

"That's just great!" Silver said. "A woman who hates guns is guarding my boat."

The crowd that had gathered began to break up. Silver lowered his gun and the man walked away. Sorry, no bloodshed today, I thought.

Silver shoved the shotgun into Doc's good hand. "When you two finish sightseeing, come on back and we'll continue our cruise." He walked away, trailed by a nervous little man carrying a toolbox.

Doc looked around the town. "What were you doing up here?"

"Just wanted to stretch my legs."

"You couldn't have picked a more depressing spot."

"You haven't seen anything," I said, and told him about the gold pit outside town and the Indian getting punched.

"That's a good way to get killed, Jake. We better get back to the boat before Captain Bligh leaves without us. I wouldn't want to be marooned here."

"Tell me about it, mister!" a man said behind us.

We turned around. The man was a little over five feet tall. He had long, curly black hair, a scraggly beard, and no front teeth.

"Didn't mean to eavesdrop," he said. "Americans?"

Doc nodded.

"Thought so. And you're new in town?"

"Just passing through."

"Are you going up- or downriver?"

"Up."

"Oh." He looked disappointed, then a thought occurred to him. "But you're coming back down. What goes up must come down." He laughed at his joke.

"We've got to get going," Doc said. We started for the path, and the man joined us.

"My name's Fred Stoats."

"Nice to meet you, Fred," Doc said. We kept walking.

"I've been stuck here for two years. Had a claim . . . Had three claims, in fact, but I lost them. Been haulin' rock sacks out of the hellhole like a monkey ever since. Trying to get enough cash together to go downriver. Got to get back to the good old U.S. of A. and see my wife and little girl. She's real sick."

Doc stopped. "Who's sick? Your wife or your little girl?"

"Little girl. Little Mary, we call her. Has cancer. I miss her."

Doc looked at him, trying to figure out if he was telling the truth.

"You need help on your boat?" Fred asked.

"I don't think so." Doc started walking again. He didn't buy Fred's story, and neither did I.

"That was a real nice thing you done for Raul," he said to me.

"Who?"

"The Indian. His name's Raul."

"Oh." We got to the top of the trail.

Jaguar

"Those guys were giving him a rough time because of the jaguar," Fred added.

This stopped us in our tracks.

"What jaguar?" Doc asked.

"Boy, you guys *are* new in town! The jaguar that's been killin' the dogs at night. The jaguar that everyone's tryin' to get their hands on for the reward and pool money."

Fred had a captive audience now. Doc's eyes were lit up like flares. We weren't going anywhere.

Fred went on to explain that one of the store owners was offering fifty dollars for the jaguar's skin. This same owner had set up a betting pool. For a dollar you could bet on the jaguar's weight. The man with the closest guess would get all the money in the pool.

"How long has the jaguar been around here?" Doc asked.

"About two months. They've tried everything to kill that devil. They've tethered goats as bait and sat in shooting blinds all night, set snares. . . . They even put out poisoned meat. Nothing's worked, although we did lose a few dogs with that poisoned-meat idea. Nobody's even seen the jaguar. It comes in like fog and leaves like smoke."

"What makes you think it's a jaguar?" Doc asked.

"Ha! Come with me." He led us back into town, and we followed him as he zigzagged between several hovels. "There!" he said, pointing to the ground.

Doc squatted down and looked at the print in the mud. "That's a jaguar, all right."

127

"That's fresh from last night."

"So what about this Raul?"

"The rumor is that he's pretty good at tracking cats. I don't know if it's true, but that's what people say. Problem is that Raul doesn't want anything to do with it. Money doesn't mean a thing to him, and he thinks the jaguar should be left alone. Those men were just trying to convince him to give them a hand when your boy came along."

"I'd like to talk to Raul," Doc said.

Fred picked at something in his beard for a moment. "Well, I could take you to him," he said. He looked at his wrist as if he were checking the time. The only problem was, he didn't have a watch on. "I've got an important appointment in a few minutes. I sure hate to miss it. I'm meetin' a guy who might just be my ticket out of here."

Doc dug into his pocket and pulled out a twenty-dollar bill. Fred snatched it out of his hand and stuffed it into his pocket before Doc could change his mind. "Raul lives down in the Indian camp. It's not far."

He led us to a trail on the other side of town. The Indians' living conditions were worse than those in town, which was hard to believe. Despite the heat, people huddled near smoking fires to keep the insects away. Potbellied children ran around completely naked. I noticed ugly red scars on their legs and arms and asked Fred what they were.

"Piranha bites," he said. "They don't eat you up like in the movies, but they can sure take out a divot of flesh if they're hungry."

"Why don't these people live in town with everyone else?"

"They have their ways and we have ours. Living separate keeps the fights down, somewhat."

It was clear that we weren't welcome. Men and women with dull, hostile expressions watched us walk by. Most of them had tattoos all over their bodies, including their faces. Almost everyone we passed had golf-ball-sized wads of tobacco or something stuffed in their cheeks. Many of them spit strings of brown juice when we walked by.

"Don't pay attention," Fred said. "It's just their way."

We came to a stop outside a lean-to built next to a tree.

"Raul!" Fred shouted, adding something in Portuguese. "He don't speak any English and only a little Portuguese."

Raul crawled out of the lean-to and sat on his haunches, looking up at us. His right eye was swollen shut. He didn't seem to recognize me. Like the other Indians, he had black tattoos on his arms and face. On either side of his upper lip he had three tattooed lines that looked like cat whiskers. Two young girls, no more than six or seven years old, peeked at us from behind the tree the lean-to was against. A couple of people sauntered over to see what was going on. They were soon joined by several others.

"Tell him that I would like his help catching the jaguar," Doc said. "Tell him that I won't kill the jaguar. I'll use a drug to make the cat go to sleep. When the jaguar wakes up, I'll let him go someplace a long way from here where it will be safe."

"That's a mouthful," Fred said, picking at his beard and looking at his wrist.

"I'll give you more money when we leave," Doc told him.

Fred pantomimed as he talked, to make sure that Raul understood. Fred seemed to have some difficulty explaining the tranquilizing and waking-up part, but managed to get through it. Raul watched him impassively. A couple of times he glanced at Doc and me.

Fred finally came to the end of his speech. Raul stared off into the distance. We waited for what seemed like a long time. No one said anything—even the spitting stopped.

Raul turned his head toward Doc and said something. He then called one of the girls out from behind the tree and whispered in her ear. She and her friend ran off giggling.

Fred shook his head. "He said, 'No.'"

"Are you sure you explained it to him right?"

"Clear as a bell. He doesn't want to help you. We better go."

Doc didn't want to leave. "Tell him that the jaguar will die unless he lets me tranquilize it."

"I already did that," Fred insisted.

"Do it again!"

Fred rolled his eyes, then said a few more words. Raul shook his head, then climbed back into his lean-to. "Sorry," Fred said. "But I still get my money."

"You'll get it."

We walked back through the camp. The spitting started
up again, and people began muttering things and snicker-
ing as we passed. I felt very uncomfortable. The Indians
probably had the same feeling every day as they walked
through the mining town on their way to the gold pit.

When we got back to the town, Doc gave Fred five dollar bill. "You sure you don't need any help on your boat?"
Fred asked. "I'd sure like to get out of here."

"I'm afraid not."

"Oh, well," Fred said. "Maybe I got the weight right on
that cat. You know, it's just as well you didn't get that jaguar.
Catching it alive wouldn't set well with most of the people
around here."

Doc and I headed to the trail leading to the docks. About
halfway down, we heard someone shouting behind us. It was
the two little girls that had been with Raul. They ran up to
us. One of them had her hands behind her back. She brought
one hand forward and presented me with a piece of string.

"What's this?"

She brought her other hand forward and released a large
metallic-blue butterfly. It was beautiful. The two girls
giggled and ran back up the path. Doc and I watched the
butterfly flutter back and forth, trying to get free.

"Morpho butterfly," Doc said.

I reached into my pocket with my free hand and took out
my pocketknife. Doc helped me cut the string, and the
morpho danced away into what was left of the forest.

CHAPTER 13

was about ready go look for you," Flanna said, when we got on board.

Doc told her what had happened.

"Are you sure this Fred explained the situation?"

Doc's understanding of Portuguese wasn't very good, but he said he thought that Raul understood. Silver came up from below for a second and got something out of the wheelhouse, then went back below without saying a word to us.

"How's the engine?" Doc asked.

"Silver and the mechanic have been arguing ever since they got down there. I feel sorry for the little man. Silver thinks we'll be under way again sometime tomorrow morning."

"Silver won't kill him. He needs him to fix the engine." Doc sat down on his hammock. Flanna took out her kit and started to change his bandage.

"I've got to do something about this jaguar," Doc told her. "The problem is time. If only we could capture it quickly. We'd learn so much by tracking it at the preserve— the jaguar would be like a guide. It's so frustrating!"

Doc wasn't frustrated. He was stimulated. This was the happiest he had been since we left Manaus.

"There's no time to put out a live trap, and I suspect the locals would tamper with it anyway," he continued. "They want the skin."

"Did you offer Raul money?"

"He doesn't seem to be interested in money."

"Perhaps I could go up and talk to him," Flanna suggested. "I know a few words of several dialects. Tranquilizing an animal is a very difficult concept to get across. He may have misunderstood."

"It might be worth a try," Doc said. "Let's get something to eat, then we'll go back up to the camp."

We didn't have to go back to the Indian camp, because Raul came to us. And he didn't come sauntering down the dock; he came from the river in a dugout canoe. While we were eating, we heard a tapping sound on the starboard side. At first we thought it was engine-repair noise from down below. The tapping got more insistent, and I took a look over the side. Raul was standing in the canoe, knocking on the hull as if it were the front door of a house.

"We have visitors," I announced.

The canoe had two other men in it. They lifted Raul onto

their shoulders so he could reach the rail. Flanna and I helped him the rest of the way up.

When he got on deck, he glanced nervously toward the dock and whispered something.

"He says that he came from the water so he wouldn't attract attention," Flanna translated. "His Portuguese is excellent."

Doc quickly pulled the mosquito netting down, and Raul began to relax, somewhat.

Raul talked quietly for several minutes. Flanna listened, asked questions, commented, smiled, and even laughed a couple of times. When he was finished, she said, "I'll give you the short version. Raul is certain he can help you capture the jaguar. He didn't tell you this afternoon because he was afraid that some of the hunters in town might try to stop him if they knew. But before he agrees, he has a couple of conditions."

"Fantastic!" Doc said. He was very excited and it was good to see.

"The first is that he wants to look at the tranquilizer darts and have you explain how they work."

"No problem."

"After you've captured the jaguar, he wants to take it to town and have it weighed."

"Why?"

"I didn't quite understand this part, but I think he wants to pacify the people in town who've entered the betting pool."

"Okay," Doc said, but he didn't like the idea. I'm sure his preference was to take the jaguar and run.

"And finally," Flanna continued, "Raul wants to go with us to the preserve and see the jaguar set free."

Doc and I were both surprised by this.

"Doesn't he trust us?" Doc asked.

"I don't think it's that."

"Does he understand that we'll be at the preserve for at least a couple of months?"

"Yes, and he still wants to go."

Doc had to think about this one for a while. "Silver's not going to like the idea, but he's not in charge of the expedition. Tell Raul that if we don't get the jaguar, he doesn't go with us."

Flanna explained.

Raul nodded, then said, "I get jaguar." I guess he spoke a little English, too.

Doc got out his tranquilizing equipment.

"You'll have to do the honors, Jake. I can't do it one-handed."

Flanna explained how it all worked as I put the darts together. The darts used for cats are about three inches long. The shaft, where the drug is held, is made out of a hollow aluminum tube threaded on the inside on both ends. The tubes are reusable. I put a rubber plunger into one end of the shaft. I then took a brass gunpowder cap about the size of a .22 and seated it in the plunger. I screwed a cap over the top of this. The end cap has a tuft of cotton sticking out from it, which is how the air rifle pushes the dart out of the barrel.

I flipped the shaft over, ready to put the tranquilizer drug into it. Flanna showed Raul the little bottle of drugs and tried to explain how it worked. He looked at the bottle carefully, obviously confused by this part of the procedure. Doc told me how much of each type of drug to put into the shaft. When it was full, I screwed the needle onto the end.

Doc showed Raul the dart rifle. Doc held his hand over the barrel and dry-fired it to prove to Raul that it was harmless without the dart in it. Raul put his own hand over the end of the barrel and nodded for Doc to pull the trigger. He smiled when he felt the puff of air come out. He said something to Flanna and she laughed.

"He said it works like a blowgun."

"Exactly."

When the demonstration was finished, Raul climbed back over the side and got into the canoe. He said that he would return sometime before sunrise the next morning.

"What are we going to tell Silver?" I asked.

"Nothing at this point," Doc said. "We'll worry about it later, *if* we capture the jaguar. The chances of that are pretty slim."

* * *

Raul showed up about half an hour before sunrise, carrying a small, dirty cotton bag over his shoulder. He handed the bag up to me and said something to Flanna.

"These are his things for the trip upriver," Flanna said.

The bag was nearly empty. I guess he believed in traveling light. I put it under my hammock.

Raul brought three canoes and three men to help us. We lowered the equipment to them quietly so we wouldn't wake Silver. I was afraid Scarlet would hear us and call out, but she must have gone on another shore leave.

Once we were in the canoes, they pushed off and started paddling against the current. It was a very dark night, and I could hardly see anything ahead of us, but the men paddling didn't seem to have a problem navigating through the darkness. The insects swarmed all around us, despite the insect repellent we had smeared on. We paddled upriver a couple of miles until we came to a small tributary. We followed the tributary for another mile, then stopped. Raul got out and motioned for us to stay in the canoes. He went off into the forest and was gone for about half an hour. By the time he returned, it was light out. He spoke to Flanna in a soft whisper.

"He says that the jaguar is a female."

"How does he know that?" Doc asked.

Flanna shrugged her shoulders. "He wants us to follow him with the rifle and darts. When we have the jaguar, he'll call the other men and they'll bring the rest of the equipment."

Raul moved through the forest with the grace of a deer.

His toes were splayed out and twisted from a lifetime of walking barefoot over uneven terrain. He came to a small open area and stopped. He whispered to Flanna.

"He wants to know who is going to dart the jaguar."

"Jake's the shooter," Doc said. "I can't do it with my bum hand."

Doc had taught me to use the dart rifle when I was a little kid.

"Okay," Flanna said. "We're to wait here and stay out of sight. Raul will position Jake up ahead and call the jaguar to him."

"He's going to call the jaguar?" Doc asked, in surprise.

"That's what he says."

"This I've got to see. You have everything, Jake."

I slipped a loaded dart into the breech of the rifle. "I'm ready."

"You'll only get one chance."

I nodded and followed Raul deeper into the forest. He stopped at the base of a huge tree and positioned me near the trunk behind a tangle of vines. He pointed to a spot about twenty feet away. I guessed this is where he thought the jaguar was going to appear. I lay down in a prone position. When I was comfortable, I flipped the safety off and brought the butt of the rifle up to my shoulder.

Raul moved off to my right, disappearing from view. For a long time nothing happened. Sweat trickled down my face. Insects buzzed all around me, and it took all my willpower to resist swatting them away. I heard a bird call to my right. I wondered when Raul was going to start. The bird called again, and I realized that Raul had already started! I didn't know what kind of bird he was imitating, but the call certainly sounded genuine.

Several minutes passed. My neck began to cramp. I started to wonder how Raul knew where the jaguar was going to appear. What if the cat came up behind me? Or over to my left? *Stop it, Jake! Think like you're stalking. Breathe. Concentrate on the spot. There's nothing but the spot. . . .* I saw a leaf move in the clump of palms in front of me. There was a shift in the forest, as if the volume had been turned down. The jaguar was here. She wanted the bird. I saw her head first—yellow fur spotted with black rosettes, bright golden eyes. Her stocky, powerful body moved low to the ground as she placed each foot with infinite care before taking the next step. I didn't move. I took long, slow breaths. I wanted to put the dart in her thick haunch muscle. *Wait for the rosette to come to you. Wait. . . .*

Pop! I hadn't consciously pulled the trigger. The sound startled me. When the dart hit, she jumped straight up and let out a chest-rattling roar. She bit angrily at the dart in her haunch, tearing it out of her leg. She licked her wound, then walked away. I waited. Five minutes passed. Someone touched me on the shoulder. Raul. I stood up and worked the kink out of my neck. Doc and Flanna came over.

"Nice shot, Jake." Doc looked at his watch. "We'll give

her a few more minutes to make sure she's completely out." Flanna told Raul what we were doing.

We found her about fifty yards away, lying on her side.

Raul's men came up with the medical kit and the stretcher to carry her back to the boat. Doc checked the jaguar's breathing and squeezed some ointment into her open eyes, so they wouldn't dry out. He looked at her teeth.

"I'd say she's four or five years old. If it is a she." He lifted her hind leg. "Damn!"

"What?"

"She has milk, which means she has cubs somewhere."

Flanna explained the situation to Raul. He nodded and took off into the forest with one of his men. About ten minutes later, Raul came back alone.

"He found the cubs," Flanna said. "He thinks there are two of them."

He led us to the den, which was under a tree near a small stream. Doc bent down and shone his flashlight inside. "Two sets of eyes. I'd guess they're three or four months old—close to being weaned. She's probably been bringing dog meat back to them for weeks. It's going to take awhile to get them out of here. Maybe we should take their mom back to the boat before she comes out of the drug, then come back and get them. We can bring some crates back to put the cubs in. I don't think they'll leave the den, but someone should stay here and make sure."

Jaguar

Flanna spoke to Raul, and he told one of his men to guard the den.

We carried the female to the canoes and paddled back to the mining settlement. As soon as we arrived the word went out and a stream of people ran down the path to see the jaguar.

Doc wanted to get her right on the boat and put her into the cage we had assembled the night before, but Raul stopped him and pointed up the path.

"You made a deal," Flanna reminded Doc.

"I know, but it doesn't make sense. The best thing for the jaguar is to get her right onto the boat." He looked at Raul. It was clear that Raul expected Doc to take the jaguar up to town. Doc sighed. "We'll have to hurry," he said. "She'll be waking up pretty soon."

Silver came walking down the dock with his shotgun. He looked at the jaguar. "I saw the cage on deck this morning," he said. "I should have known it was something like this."

He only knew one third of it.

"We have to take her up to be weighed," Doc said. He explained the deal he had made with Raul, leaving out the part about Raul coming with us.

Silver shook his head. "You know, Doc, this isn't a movie and the men up in town aren't actors. They're very real and they're not going to be happy about Doctor Dolittle taking their fun away."

"I know."

"Well, as long as you know. At least the engine is working, so we can get out of here reasonably quickly. Let's get this over with."

"You're coming with us?" Doc asked.

"Dead passengers would be very bad for my reputation."

"Who'll guard the boat?" Flanna asked.

"Our friendly little mechanic is still down there. He knows better than to let anyone on board, and I haven't paid him yet, which should keep him on our side for the time being."

We walked up the path with a parade of people behind us. There was a huge crowd waiting inside the store, spilling out into the street. We had to push our way through the entrance and up to the weight scale. Behind the scale was a long blackboard with names and numbers. Hanging on a hook above the board was a three-gallon bucket filled with money. The store owner came over and looked at the jaguar. He jumped backward.

"He just discovered that your jaguar is still alive," Silver said, grinning. He seemed to be enjoying himself.

The owner started shouting at Raul.

"He's not pleased about losing out on the skin," Silver interpreted. "And he's blaming Raul because he led you to the jaguar. Bad day in Mudville. Go ahead and put her on the scale and let's get out of here."

Doc and I put her on the scale, and the owner moved the counterweights to balance the arm. He took his time about it, nudging the smallest weight on the arm little by little. The room got very quiet. Most of the men stared intently at the scales, hoping their number would come up. Fred Stoats stared at Flanna with his toothless mouth hanging open. The owner was finally satisfied with the weight and wrote it down on a piece of paper. He announced the weight in Portuguese, then turned to the board and ran his finger down the list of names and numbers, stopping at seventy-two kilos.

"Raul," the owner said, quietly.

Fred Stoats tore up his mark and threw it on the floor in disgust. He leaned over and hissed in my ear: "You should have taken me upriver! You're going to regret it now." He stamped out of the store.

"You better get your jaguar out of here, Doc," Silver said. "I have a feeling that things are about to get very ugly."

No wonder Raul had insisted we take the jaguar up to be weighed. He was more interested in money than we had thought.

Doc and I rolled the jaguar onto the stretcher. Raul stepped forward and gave the store owner his mark, then held his hand out for the bucket. The owner took the bucket down, but hesitated in handing it over to him.

Silver said something to the owner. I don't know what it was, but men immediately got as far away from Silver as they could. The owner's face turned bright red.

"Do you have the cat?" Silver asked, without taking his

eyes off the owner. Flanna and I picked the stretcher up.

"We're all going to leave together," Silver said. "You and your pet first, then me and your friend, Raul, with his bucket of money." He said something to the owner and punctuated it by pumping a shell into the chamber of his shotgun. The owner very reluctantly handed the bucket to Raul. "The party's over. Let's move out."

I backed out the door with the stretcher. Doc was behind me, clearing the way. When we got outside, I turned around so I could see where I was going. We walked over to the path and started down.

"Doc," Silver yelled. "Why don't you run ahead and get the mooring ropes untied. As soon as they gather their wits, they'll be coming down. I'd like to be gone when they get there."

Doc ran ahead of us. I glanced behind. Silver was walking backward down the trail. Raul walked next to him with his bucket. A group of men were following, but they kept their distance. The jaguar lifted her head for a second, then put it back down. She was coming out of the drug. When we got down to the dock, we started moving faster. By the time we got to the boat, Doc had the lines untied. We got the jaguar aboard. Silver scrambled up to the wheel house, ignoring the mechanic's complaints about getting his money. The engine came to life, and we started backing out.

When we got far enough away from the dock, Silver swung the bow around and started upriver at a pretty good clip. We put the jaguar in the cage. After a while, Silver came down from the wheelhouse to take a look at our new passenger.

The jaguar snarled at him. "She doesn't look very grateful, Doc."

Doc looked up at him. "Thanks for your help, Silver."

"All part of the service." Silver grinned. "To tell you the truth, I sort of enjoyed it, but let's not do it again. We'll drop Raul and the mechanic off upriver. Raul is going to have to stay out of town, but he'll be able to go anywhere he wants with the money he won."

"He's coming with us," Doc said.

Silver stopped grinning. "Why?"

"He wants to see the jaguar set free. Also, he happens to be the best cat tracker I've ever seen. I need him."

"Doc, Indians are the most unreliable people on earth. He won't stick around. He'll just take off one day without a word. They always do."

I thought about Silver's wife, Alicia, and his son, Tito.

"He can leave whenever he wants," Doc said.

"So now I have an Indian and a jaguar to worry about. What's next?"

"Three jaguars," I said.

Doc told him about the two cubs. When he finished, it started to rain.

Silver looked up at the sky. "I should change the boat's name to *Silver's Ark*." He walked back up to the wheelhouse.

"He took that better than I expected," Doc said.

* * *

The jaguar cubs were much bigger than Doc had predicted. They put up quite a fight as I used a noose pole to pull them out of the den. I was surprised to see that one of them was black and one was spotted.

"Black jaguars aren't that unusual," Doc said. "The black fur is called melanism. It's just a color phase. If the sun hits the fur just right, you can still see the outlines of spots."

We paddled back to the boat and handed the crates up to Silver and Flanna. When we got back on board, we helped the mechanic into one of the canoes. Raul then took his bucket of money and lowered it over the side to one of the men, and said something to him.

Silver looked very surprised.

"Raul told his friend to give the money to the people in the Indian camp," Flanna explained.

"I wouldn't have bet on that," Silver said. He said something to Raul in Portuguese, then went back up to the wheelhouse.

Flanna smiled. "Our captain just told Raul that he was welcome on his boat anytime."

"I guess there's hope for this expedition yet," Doc said. "Let's get a cage put together for the cubs."

"Why don't we put them in with their mother?" Flanna asked.

"It would be too crowded. They're ready to be weaned, anyway."

We assembled another cage and set it right next to the female's cage, so the cubs could at least see their mother.

"Our biggest problem is going to be feeding them," Doc said. "Their favorite food is the peccary and capybara, but they'll eat just about anything they can catch—turtles, deer, monkeys, sloths, snakes, lizards, caiman, birds, opossum, fish, and even snails and insects."

"Perhaps Raul is as good a hunter as he is a tracker," Flanna said.

"Let's hope so."

That night, Doc's mood was still upbeat. He had three jaguars, and he hadn't even gotten to the preserve yet.

Flanna removed his bandage. "I think the burns are finally starting to heal," she told him. "There'll be some small scars, but I think they'll go away with time."

I stood up suddenly, startling both Doc and Flanna.

"Did something bite you?" Doc asked.

"No, just feeling restless. I think I'll go up and talk to Silver for a while."

In all the excitement I had forgotten to tell Silver about the man with the scar. I climbed the stairs to the wheelhouse. He was standing at the helm with Scarlet perched on his shoulder.

"What's up?" He, too, seemed pretty cheerful.

"I forgot to tell you that I thought I saw the man with the scar in town yesterday. At least I think it was him. He was standing near the trail, looking at the *Tito* through binoculars."

Silver didn't say anything for a few moments. "Facial scars are almost as common as ears in this country. And it's very unlikely that the same guy would be way up here."

"Maybe he followed us."

"He already went through the boat. Why would he follow us? Forget about it, Jake."

"What about him watching us through binoculars?"

"I'm sure someone in town checks out every new boat that comes in. It's not the same guy."

I didn't push the issue any further, but there was a definite change in Silver's mood. The cheerfulness of a few seconds ago was gone.

"Is there anything else?" he asked, staring out the window.

"I guess not," I said, and left him alone.

When I got back to my hammock, there was something sitting on my pillow. It was wrapped in a green leaf.

"What's this?"

"I don't know," Doc said. "Raul put it there."

I looked over at Raul. He was watching the jaguars.

I opened the leaf. Inside was a large yellowed canine tooth. It had a small hole drilled in one end of it. I showed it to Doc.

"Jaguar," Doc said.

I looked back at Raul. He was watching me and said something to Flanna.

"He says it's to make you strong."

I smiled at him. He nodded and turned back to the

jaguars. I took off my snake amulet, ran the leather thong through the tooth, then put it on. I went over to Raul and showed him the tooth around my neck. He nodded with approval. I pulled out my pocketknife and gave it to him. He tried to give it back, but I folded his rough, copper-colored fingers around the knife and shook my head.

That night, Silver didn't let the anchors down. When Doc asked him why, Silver said he wanted to push upriver to make up for the lost time.

CHAPTER 14

The next few days were relatively calm. Raul spent most of his time sitting in a folding chair staring at the shoreline. I gave him a pair of binoculars to use. He could hardly keep them away from his eyes. At night he slept on the hard deck, just out of reach of the young jaguars. When Raul wasn't looking through the binoculars, he was looking over Doc's shoulder, while Flanna tried to explain what Doc was doing. Raul was enthralled with anything that had to do with technology, like Doc's laptop computer and the radio collars. Flanna joked that if we were on the boat much longer, Raul might become a computer nerd.

Raul also spent a lot of time with Silver up in the wheelhouse talking late into the night. They seemed to enjoy each other's company, which surprised all of us.

Doc's mood held up. He was excited about the preserve and the work ahead. He spent hours looking at the jaguars, and they spent hours looking at us. He built special radio collars for the two cubs. The battery pack was smaller, and the collars were made out of light canvas instead of the heavy canvas he was using on the big jaguars. His plan was to put the collars on when we got to the refuge.

"The reason I'm using the light canvas is because the cubs are still growing," he explained. "We'll try to recapture them in a couple of months and put on bigger collars. If we fail to capture them, these light collars will rot and fall off before they constrict their necks."

We named the jaguars. Well, actually Doc let me name them. The black cub was Wild Bill, after Bill Brewster. The spotted cub was Taw. And I named their mother, Beth, after my mom. Doc thought the names were perfect.

When we anchored at night, Raul gathered food for the jaguars. Sometimes he'd spear fish in the shallow water alongshore. Other times he'd go deep into the forest to hunt. He had made a bow as tall as he was and several arrows that were nearly as long as the bow. He rarely came back empty-handed. Once he brought back two howler monkeys. Another time he brought back a capybara—a rodent the size of a small dog. On his last hunting trip he hit the jackpot and bagged a tapir, which provided several hundred pounds of meat. Flanna and I had to help him carry the tapir back to the boat and put it into the cooler. Doc thought it would keep the jaguars' stomachs full until we got to the preserve.

The farther upriver we got, the fewer settlements there

were. We also started seeing a lot more wildlife, especially in the early morning and late evening. We saw troops of howler and woolly monkeys scurrying through the canopy alongshore. Giant river otters slid off the muddy banks and swam out to the boat to check us out. Flanna said the otters were called "jaguars of the river" because of their voracious appetites and skill at catching fish. Once in a while we saw an anaconda swim by, or passed a tree boa sunning itself on a branch. And of course there were countless birds darting in and out of the green tangle of trees and plants growing onshore. I think my favorite animals were the *boutos,* or Amazon dolphins. They had pinkish skin and long beaks and rode our bow waves for miles as we made our way upriver to the preserve.

One night while we were anchored, Silver took the Zodiac out by himself. He took off upriver with Scarlet flying above him and screaming her lungs out. He didn't get back until long after dark. We were all worried about him.

When we asked him what had taken him so long, he said that he had had a little motor trouble. "Took awhile to get it going. No big deal."

Before Silver went up to the wheelhouse, Doc asked him when he thought we were going to arrive at the preserve.

"Within a week," he said, confidently.

The next morning Silver pulled the anchors up very early. We had gone maybe ten miles upriver when he slowed the *Tito* down, took a hard left, and gunned the engine. Raul fell out of his chair. At first we thought Silver had done it to avoid a floating tree, but nothing passed by us and he continued heading toward the shore.

Doc and I climbed up to the wheelhouse to find out what was going on.

"What are you doing, Silver?" Doc asked.

"Shortcut," Silver said, continuing his heading. "And I thought we had an agreement that I was the captain."

"I'm not disputing that," Doc said. "I just want to know what's going on."

We were about thirty feet from shore. Silver slowed the boat down, then dropped the bow anchor to hold us in place.

"You see that tributary?" He pointed to an opening along-shore. It was barely wide enough for the *Tito* to squeeze through.

Silver went into his cabin and brought a map out. "Let's pretend for a moment that the Amazon River is an inter-state freeway, because in a sense that's what it is. It's the main highway through the Amazon Basin. Now, up here, right along the highway, is your preserve." He pointed to a large area marked in red. "And here is where you wanted to set up your base camp." There was a black *X*. "Are you with me?"

"I'm with you," Doc said. "But I still don't know where you're going."

"If you had the choice of releasing jaguars in the center of a national forest or near a freeway off-ramp, which would you choose?"

"The center, of course."

"Well, I think I have a way of getting us right to the center. You can't get there overland. There are too many swamps and other obstacles. I suspect the jaguars you want to catch and collar aren't living next to the freeway, either. They're here." He pointed to the center of the preserve.

"So how do we get there by boat?"

Silver pointed to a squiggly blue line.

"That tributary doesn't even reach the border of the preserve!" Doc protested.

"I think it does."

"You said you hadn't been in this area before. How could you possibly know that?"

"I don't," Silver admitted. "But I think it's worth a try."

"Based on what?"

"A hunch, Doc. Do you ever get those?"

Doc nodded. He was the king of hunches. "But we're supposed to meet Buzz and Woolcott up here." Doc pointed to the agreed-upon spot for the base camp.

"We have several weeks before we have to be there. If I'm right, by the time they show up, we'll have already explored the interior of the preserve. Your three cats will be miles away from civilization and safe. And I'll bet you'll have several more jaguars radio-collared."

Doc looked at the entrance to the narrow tributary. "It

doesn't look wide enough for the boat."

"It's tight," Silver admitted. "But it gets wider about a mile in. I took the Zodiac up there last night. If I'm wrong and the tributary stops, we'll turn around and continue with our original plan. We'll only lose a few days, which I think we can afford, since you already have three jaguars in hand."

"Let's get Flanna up here," Doc said.

When she got there, Silver explained the plan again. Flanna was willing, but she was suspicious of Silver's motivation. "Why would you risk your boat to do this?"

"First of all," he said, "we're not going to lose the boat. If it doesn't work out, we will lose some time and some blood—the insects are really bad up there. Second, I want to see if I'm right. And third, even if I'm wrong, I want to see what's up there."

"Curiosity," Flanna said.

Silver nodded.

* * *

It was worse than any of us could have imagined. Silver was right: the tributary did get wider about a mile up, but not by much. The branches from the trees on both sides scraped the side of the boat. Twice, snakes dropped onto the deck. Raul scooped them into the water as casually as if he were dropping a banana peel overboard.

In some places the branches met in the middle overhead, nearly blocking out all the sunlight. The main channel twisted and turned in impossible ways. We hit so many floating trees that Scarlet gave up warning Silver altogether.

But the worst of it was the insects. Black clouds of gnats, mosquitoes, and blackflies engulfed the boat. They were so thick on the outside of our mosquito netting that we couldn't see through it.

The jaguars started to go crazy. We had to leave the safety of our mosquito netting and put netting over their cages. When the net was set, Doc used two cans of repellent to kill the insects trapped inside.

Throughout the day we lay in our hammocks trying not to scratch the red, itchy welts covering our bodies. The only one who didn't seem bothered by our situation was Raul. He sat in a folding chair and flipped through *National Geographic* magazines as if he were on the deck of a luxury liner.

That night, Silver turned on bright floodlights and continued up the tributary.

The next morning, Doc and I made a dash for the wheelhouse to bring Silver some food and see if he needed us to take over the helm, so he could rest. He looked absolutely terrible. His face was swollen with bites, and he was so exhausted he could barely keep his eyes open. Even Scarlet looked tired.

"We need to turn back," Doc said.

Silver nodded wearily. "I think you're right. But the only way we can do it is to back our way out of here, which isn't going to be easy. I can steer the boat from the deck wheel, but someone's going to have to sit in the stern and give me directions."

Doc went first. He wore a long-sleeve shirt, gloves, and a special hat with mosquito netting to protect his face and neck. We also put netting around the deck wheel to shield Silver from the insects, which made it very difficult for him to see out.

Doc shouted out instructions: *Hard right! Center! That's good! Left! Stop! Center!* for two hours. It was very slow going. As Flanna got ready to relieve Doc, we heard a loud screeching sound and the engine came to a sudden stop.

Silver swore and disappeared below deck to the engine room. He came back up with very bad news.

CHAPTER 15

"We no longer have a reverse gear," Silver said.

"Can it be fixed?" Flanna asked.

"I'm afraid not. At least not here."

"So what do we do?" Doc asked.

"Follow the tributary and hope there's a place to turn around up ahead."

"And if there isn't?"

"There has to be."

Silver climbed up to the wheelhouse and started the boat back up the tributary.

* * *

By the next morning nothing had changed. If anything, the tributary had narrowed. Doc and I went up to the wheelhouse to relieve Silver at the helm. He had been up all night, and he didn't resist when Doc suggested that we take over for a while.

I led Silver to the cot in his cabin. Scarlet followed us

and landed on her perch.

"This is all my fault," Silver said.

I told him that it wasn't, but I don't think he heard me before he fell asleep.

Doc was sitting in the captain's chair with his good hand resting on the helm. Insects bounced against the windshield, trying desperately to get inside for a bite to eat.

"I'm sorry I got you into this, Jake," Doc said. "I should have insisted that you go back."

"I didn't want to go back."

"I know."

I had been waiting to ask him this question for weeks. And I knew that now wasn't the best time to get into it with him, but he was the one who brought it up. "Why didn't you want me down here with you?"

"Because of situations like this," Doc said, pointing up ahead. "The danger . . ."

"There's more to it than that!"

Doc nodded. "You're right," he said, softly. "There's a lot more."

I waited and I started to feel guilty for pushing the issue. Doc was tired and he was scared. *I* was scared. "Maybe we should talk about this later," I said.

"No. You've been waiting long enough. I just don't know if I can explain it. I'm not sure if I understand what's going on myself."

"You don't have to, Doc."

"I'll try," he said. "When we came back from Kenya and moved to Poughkeepsie, I thought that everything would be fine. That I'd work on my field notes and you'd go to school. In the summer, maybe we'd take off and go someplace and come back in the fall so you could go back to school. That was the plan, anyway. But after a month I started to feel restless, and I knew it wasn't going to work." He looked at me. "To tell you the truth, Jake. If Bill hadn't called with this field project, I would have tried to get a project of my own."

"You mean you would have left me behind?"

"Yes," he said. "I think I would have."

I let this sink in for a minute, and it didn't feel very good. "I thought we were partners."

"This is where it gets confusing for me. I was trying to be a good father and a good field biologist. I now realize that doing both at the same time may not be possible.

"Your mom understood this. That's why she stayed at the university and didn't go into the field. She was the one making sure you got to school, that you went to the doctor and dentist, and that you had someone to talk to when you had a problem. She loved you very, very much. You are who you are because of Beth, not because of me. I let you down, Jake. And I let her down, too."

I started to protest, but he stopped me.

"If we get out of this, we're going back to Poughkeepsie."

"But your work . . ."

"No," he interrupted. "It's time I started acting like your

father. The work can wait. You'll be out of high school in three years. That leaves plenty of time for me to get back into the field. Beth wanted you to have a formal education. You can't get one down here. I want to complete what she started. I owe her that. You're the best work we ever did. Beth saw to that, and I wish she were here so I could tell her."

I started to cry. I couldn't help myself. My father joined me.

"If only Silver could see us now," I said.

Doc laughed and wiped his tears away. "Yeah, he'd be real impressed."

"I don't think you'll be happy in Poughkeepsie," I said.

"Poughkeepsie looks pretty good right now."

I had to agree with him on this, but I knew Doc well enough to realize that his resolve could change overnight. All it would take was another field project, another animal in trouble, and he would be gone.

"What about Flanna?"

"I'm sorry I didn't tell you about her before you got down here. I should have. In fact, Flanna asked me to, but I didn't know what to say, or how you would take it. It was selfish of me."

"So you love her?"

"I think so, but I don't know where it's going to take us. She's a remarkable woman. I'm not sure she deserves to be stuck with someone like me."

"She could do a lot worse."

"She could also do a lot better."

"I like her," I told him, and I meant it.

"I'm glad to hear that, Jake."

A few hours later, Doc asked me to go below and get one of the handheld global positioning units we had on board. I brought it up and turned it on, but I had to wait for an opening before I could get a hit off one of the satellites orbiting thousands of miles above us. After I got the reading, Doc had me take the wheel, so he could calculate where we were on the map.

"Silver's hunch was right," he said. "We're miles from where the tributary ends on the map. We've crossed the preserve boundary and we're headed toward the center in a roundabout way. Not that it will do us much good."

"I think it will open up," Silver said from behind us.

We turned around. He didn't look much better after four hours of sleep.

"What makes you think so?" Doc asked.

"Because I was right about the tributary leading to the center of the preserve," he said, but he didn't look all that confident.

We stared at the map as if it might help us in some mysterious way.

* * *

That afternoon, Silver called all of us into the wheelhouse to discuss our options. As we talked, he continued to steer the boat upstream.

Doc wanted to know if we could widen the channel and make our own turnaround.

"We'd bottom out in the shallows," Silver said.

"What about taking the Zodiac back down to the river and getting help?" Flanna suggested.

"We're beyond help up here," Silver said. "Any boat big enough to pull us out would find itself in the same situation as we are." He paused, as if he were reconsidering the idea. "I guess we could start ferrying people down to the river. The Zodiac will carry three of us. It would be a hellish trip, but at least . . ."

Scarlet screamed and started hitting the window with her beak. Silver quickly reduced power. All of us looked out the window, trying to see what she was so upset about. We couldn't see anything. Just the same narrow channel crowded with vegetation and trees. There was nothing blocking our way.

"What's gotten into you?" Silver asked. Scarlet started screaming even louder and hit the glass so hard I thought it would break. Silver slid the side window open and Scarlet took off through it as if she were being chased by a harpy eagle. She flew straight down the channel and disappeared around the bend.

"I guess she didn't like the idea of us using the Zodiac to get out of here," Silver said. "I can't say that I blame her."

I stared out through the open window and what I *didn't*

see amazed me. "The insects are gone," I said. They weren't totally gone, but there were several million fewer than there had been a few minutes earlier.

Flanna put her hand outside. When she pulled it back in, there were only half a dozen gnats and mosquitoes crawling on it. "Now that's what I call an improvement," she said.

Silver eased the boat around the next bend. "Well, I'll be . . ."

About three hundred yards in front of us was an opening with bright light shining through it. We stared in stunned silence as it drew nearer. When we passed through, we found ourselves on a small lake. Silver cut the engine and started the anchors down.

Everyone stepped out of the wheelhouse. In front of us was a sheer, rocky wall about thirty feet high. A waterfall poured down from the top. Clinging to the side of the wall was a flock of red and yellow macaws. When they saw the boat, they took off, disappearing into the green canopy surrounding the little lake. All but one, that is . . . Scarlet still clung to the wall, wondering why her new friends had abandoned her. To the left of the wall was a sandy beach.

Flanna, Doc, and I hugged each other.

"I knew it was here!" Silver said. "I just knew it!"

The only one of us who didn't seem surprised or moved by the discovery was Raul. He went to the back of the boat to get the binoculars and started scanning the shore.

Silver checked one of the anchor cables. "It's deep," he

said. "It must be some kind of natural sinkhole."

Doc went to the wheelhouse and brought back the map and the global positioning system. He got a reading immediately and marked a small red circle on the map. The lake was almost exactly in the center of the preserve.

He looked up at Silver. "That was some hunch," he said.

Silver was too excited to respond.

The
Preserve

CHAPTER 16

"The jaguars are free," Doc said. "Over."

"Roger. I'm switching to telemetry mode. Out." I dropped the Morpho's left wing and started slowly circling eight hundred feet above the canopy. I dialed in Beth's frequency. When I picked up the steady *beep . . . beep . . . beep* from her radio collar, I marked her position with the GPS and wrote the location down in the notebook Doc had given me. Next I dialed in Wild Bill's collar, then Taw's. The three jaguars were together under the umbrella of rain forest canopy.

I flipped the switch back to radio. "They're all coming in loud and clear."

"Great!" Doc said. "Raul and I are going to do some exploring. We should be back later this afternoon, or early this evening. Out."

It was a beautiful day despite the intense heat. As I flew back toward camp, I again tried to see the tributary we had taken

169

to get to the lake. It was nowhere in sight. The canopy completely covered it. No wonder it wasn't shown on the map. We all referred to it as the tunnel now. None of us were looking forward to going back through it when the time came.

We had been at the lake for two weeks. It took us three days to set up camp, and five days for me to get the Morpho back together. It would have taken a lot longer if Silver hadn't helped me.

The spot we picked for camp was about two hundred feet in from shore under the rain forest canopy. We put up four tents—one for Doc and Flanna, one for me, a cook tent, and a tent for our gear. Silver slept on the boat in his cabin. The boat was anchored on the far side of the lake, near the tunnel, so I'd have enough room to take off and land the Morpho. Silver used the Zodiac to get to it.

Raul built a lean-to out of large palms near the edge of camp. We told him that we had a tent for him, but he wasn't interested. There was another thing he wasn't interested in, either—clothes. The first day we got to the lake, he took his off and hadn't put them on since. The only thing he wore was the cotton bag slung over his shoulder. It was a little strange having him running around naked, but we got used to it after a few days.

Raul continued to give me little presents. There was a flat rock next to the waterfall that I sat on during the heat of the day to cool off, and, from time to time, he would leave me gifts up there. So far he had given me the jaguar tooth, various feathers, a turtle skull, a blue stone, and a dried piranha jaw. I never thanked him for the gifts. Instead, I'd leave a gift for him on the rock in exchange. I had given him the pocketknife, a mini-flashlight, a pair of pliers, and a five-dollar bill, which was worthless, but it's all I had at the time.

Flanna was in botanical heaven. We hadn't been out of the boat for ten minutes before she was up in a tree, crawling around in the canopy looking things over. She set up a canopy research station about half a mile from camp. She spent all day up there and, sometimes, all night.

Doc had slipped back into his usual intense self. He was up before the howler monkeys let loose with their morning serenade. He would slurp down a cup of coffee, pack his gear, and disappear into the rain forest with Raul at his side. Going back to Poughkeepsie was the furthest thing from his mind, which didn't surprise me.

With Raul's help, he had already captured one anteater, three monkeys, two capybaras, one paca, one tapir, and a number of other small mammals. Most of the animals were radio-collared and set free. The animals that were too small to be radio-collared were either tagged or tattooed. Doc wanted to know what types of animals were out in the forest, how they utilized the forest, and how they interacted with one another.

He was also running telemetry trials—trying to determine the effectiveness of radio tracking from the ground with a handheld antenna and receiver. One problem with air-tracking is that on some days you simply can't fly because of weather or mechanical problems. Doc found out that the new ground tracking equipment we had would pick up a collar from about five miles away, and sometimes further, depending on the terrain and where the animal was hanging out. He was quite pleased with the results, because it meant we could effectively track on the ground when the Morpho couldn't fly.

At night, Doc would come stumbling back into camp totally exhausted and spend hours entering data into his laptop computer.

Flanna and I were concerned about how hard he was pushing himself. He wasn't drinking enough water or eating enough food, he slept about four hours a night, and he paid absolutely no attention to our advice. He wanted this preserve for the animals and the rain forest, but, most of all, he wanted it for Bill Brewster. He wasn't about to let his human frailties stand in the way of fulfilling his friend's dream. The dream was driving him to his limits.

After his initial excitement over finding the lake, Silver became edgy again. He wanted everyone to keep the shotguns handy, but Flanna and Doc absolutely refused this time around. They were no longer on the boat, and Silver was no longer their captain. Silver stuck very close to camp during the first few days. At night I'd see him sitting on the deck of the boat, staring out across the lake.

After about a week his attitude changed. He began taking short trips into the rain forest by himself. As the days went by, the trips got longer and longer. He became almost as driven as Doc, but I had no idea why. He would leave for a day or two at a time, come dragging back into camp covered in sweat and grime, then take the Zodiac out to the boat. When I asked him where he went, he'd say he was just out for a relaxing little stroll. He didn't look relaxed to me.

And Scarlet? She spent most of her time with her new feathered friends doing whatever macaws do in the rain forest. The only time she came to camp was when the flock visited the lake, and she never stayed long. When the flock flew away, she was right in the middle of it.

As for me, I spent as much time as possible flying above the canopy in the Morpho. I took the ultralight up twice a day, weather permitting, to get locations on the collared animals.

Doc had waited to release the jaguars until he had a better understanding of the area. Now that they were free, tracking would be a lot more interesting.

* * *

This was by far the clearest day I had flown, and I wasn't eager to get back to camp. Every time I went up, I'd try to pick a different route back to the lake, but I didn't detour too much out of the way because we were low on gas and couldn't afford to waste it.

Jaguar

Landing in the lake was easy compared to landing on the river. There was very little crosswind and the current was slow. The only thing I had to watch out for was the pair of dolphins that showed up periodically in the lake. Fortunately, they had learned to dive into the depths when they heard the Morpho's engine.

I taxied to the beach, cut the engine, then jumped out and pulled the Morpho up on the sand. I put a tarp over it to protect the fabric from deteriorating in the sun.

I didn't expect anyone to be at camp, but now that the jaguars had been set free, it seemed more deserted than normal. Up until today, the cats had kept me company during the long wait between flights.

I went over to Doc's tent and transferred the coordinates from the morning's flight into his logbook. When he got back this evening, he would enter the data into his computer. This was all I had to do until late afternoon, when I'd take my second flight.

I put my shorts on, grabbed a towel, and headed down to the rock. When I got there, I found yet another gift from Raul. It was some kind of nutshell with geometric designs carved in it. He must have carved it with the knife I'd given him. I felt in my pocket and found an automatic pencil. It wasn't much, but it was better than a five-dollar bill. I was running out of things to leave for him.

I lay back and let the mist from the waterfall cool me off. Doc had been so preoccupied we hadn't had a chance to continue the conversation we had in the boat on the way through the tunnel, but I had thought about it a lot. There was no way he was going to be satisfied in Poughkeepsie. Wandering around wild places was as important to his life as breathing was to other people. *"He's a man who needs to be out in the wilderness howling at the moon."* In Poughkeepsie, people were arrested for that kind of behavior.

I had no doubt that when Woolcott saw what Doc had accomplished in such a short time, Bill's dream was going to come true. Then what? Doc would say good-bye to Brazil and Flanna, and he and I would live happily ever after in our ranch house in Poughkeepsie? I didn't think so. No, Doc was going to have to come up with a different solution. And the only way I could see to resolve the problem was to have me stay down here with him. At least I hoped that's the way it would turn out.

Then there was Taw—I'd miss him. And I'd promised him the Arizona trip. I didn't know if he was serious about this, or whether he would even remember that he wanted me to go there with him. But if this was something he wanted to do, I'd feel bad about letting him down.

* * *

Late that afternoon I took off in the Morpho again. Surprisingly, Beth was no longer near her cubs. She was at least five miles away from them, and seemed to be moving even farther away. Doc said Taw and Wild Bill were big enough to be on their own, but he thought Beth would stick close to them for a few weeks or months.

I flew over them again and double-checked the readings. The cats had definitely split up. I tried to get Doc on the radio, but he didn't answer. He must have turned his handset off.

I turned the Morpho around and flew back to the lake.

Doc and Raul didn't get back to camp until after dark. I told Doc about the jaguars not being together anymore.

"That's interesting," he said wearily, looking at the logbook. He got his laptop out of the tent and retrieved a fresh battery from the charger plugged into the small generator we had brought with us.

"How about some food, Bob?" Flanna said.

"I'm not really hungry."

"I think you should eat, anyway," she said, firmly.

"I'm not hungry!"

"Suit yourself."

Doc took a deep breath. "I'm sorry, Flanna. I didn't mean to snap at you. I guess I'm just tired."

"You need to take a couple of days off," she said. "Your arm was badly burned and you've been under a lot of stress. You're pushing yourself too hard."

"The arm is just fine." He held it up and flexed his fingers. The bandage had been off for a week.

Flanna looked at him doubtfully.

"Raul found some old jaguar sign today," Doc said. "We're going to head out tomorrow and see if we can find it. . . . Or him. Raul says it's a male. We'll only be gone a few days. . . ."

"A few days!" Flanna was irritated, and I didn't blame her. Doc was in no shape to go traipsing off into the forest for several days.

"It might only take a couple of days," he said. "We need to get more jaguars collared."

"You're being foolish, Bob!" Flanna was really mad now, and I admired her for it. "You should take a week off and do nothing but sleep."

"I'll rest after we leave here," he said. "I feel just fine." He got up and went into his tent. Flanna followed him.

I heard them talking late into the night. I hoped that Flanna would talk some sense into him.

CHAPTER 17

She hadn't. The next morning Doc was up at his usual time, stuffing his pack with gear. He didn't look healthy. "Doc, are you feeling all right?"

"I'm fine," he said, and tried to smile. "If the weather isn't right, don't go up."

"Flanna's right," I said. "You should wait until you're stronger."

"Jake, I have to do this. I promise I'll take it easy out there. Don't worry about me."

"Right." An idea occurred to me. "Why don't you let me go with you? I could carry some of the gear—lighten your load."

"You need to stay here and keep track of the jaguars. I'm concerned that Beth isn't near her cubs. Something isn't right."

"What will you do if she stays away from them?"

"Probably nothing."

"Then why don't you let me go with you?"

"Jake, your job is to fly the Morpho. I'll be fine." He gave me a halfhearted hug and slipped his pack over his shoulders. A few moments later, he and Raul disappeared behind a veil of green vegetation.

Flanna came out of the tent after he had left. "Your father is the most pigheaded man I've ever known!"

I laughed.

"What's so funny?" she snapped.

"You sound exactly like someone else I used to know." I don't know how many times I had heard my mom say the same thing, with exactly the same level of exasperation.

She took a deep breath. "He's a maniac!"

"But you gotta love him."

"That's the worst part! He's been running a fever for the past week. He thinks he can *work* his way through it." She shook her head. "Oh, well, we tried. . . . Are you ready to learn something about climbing trees?"

"Absolutely!"

"Great. When you come back from your morning flight, I'll show you my web."

"What web?"

"You'll see."

* * *

Wild Bill and Taw were in the same areas I had found them in the day before. Beth was another story. I circled around and around trying to pick up her signal, with no luck. I began to wonder if her collar had malfunctioned. I flew around some more, then started to get low on gas. I continued to monitor her frequency as I flew back toward the lake. About halfway there, I picked up a faint signal. It grew louder the closer I got to the lake, and still louder as I passed over the lake. What was she up to? I finally flew over the top of her several miles west of the lake. At this rate she would be out of the Morpho's range in a few days. I hoped she would settle down.

By the time I landed, I was nearly on empty. I reminded myself to be more careful in the future. Doc wouldn't be very happy if I had to tell him that I lost the Morpho because I ran out of gas. To say nothing about what Buzz would say when we finally saw him again.

Silver was standing on the shore. He must have just gotten back from one of his strolls. He looked worn out, but he helped me put the Morpho away.

"So you let the jaguars go?"

"Yesterday, and Beth is in a traveling mode." I told him where she was.

"What's it like on that side of the lake?"

"What do you mean?"

"I don't know," he said. "Did you see any unusual land formations, other lakes? Things like that."

I shook my head. "Just green canopy. Are you looking for something in particular?"

"Nah. I'm just interested in the geography of this place.

If you're over there again, keep your eyes open and let me know if you see anything."

"Sure."

I told him that Doc and Raul had taken off for a few days. He seemed too tired to care one way or the other. He got into the Zodiac and headed out to the *Tito*.

Before I visited Flanna, I went up to the rock to make sure Raul had picked up the mechanical pencil. I didn't want it to rust while he was away. It was gone.

* * *

I took the trail to Flanna's treetop kingdom. In the few areas where the sunlight found its way through the thick canopy, there were patches of dense tropical growth. But very little sunlight made it to the ground. Most of the light was blocked a hundred feet above, where the lowest tree branches hung.

I came across a river of red flower petals crossing the trail in front of me. A two-inch-wide column of leaf-cutting ants were carrying petals to their underground nest. I had read that their nests were gigantic, holding up to five million workers. The entrances to the same nest can be separated by as much as fifty yards. The ants don't eat the leaves or petals. They use them to cultivate subterranean fungus gardens.

I stepped over the column and continued on. The huge tree trunks I passed were covered with moss and plants. Aerial roots twisted around each other and dangled to the ground.

When I got to the site, I didn't see Flanna. I put my head

all the way back and tried to find her in the dark canopy, but I couldn't spot her. I called out.

"I'll be there in a second!" Flanna called back.

A few moments later, she dropped to the ground on the end of a rope. She had on a yellow hard hat, gloves, a pair of protective goggles hanging around her neck, and a machete hanging from a belt around her waist. It reminded me of old photos I had seen of Taw in his steelworking outfit—minus the machete.

Flanna gave me about an hour of climbing instructions before she let me put the harness on.

"How do you get the first rope up in the tree?" I asked.

"If there are good vines around the trunk, I free-climb. If not, I use a bow and arrow.

She brought out a compound bow and a quiver of arrows. "I don't use the points, of course."

She took an arrow, removed the point, and put on a different attachment. She tied some heavy fishing line to the attachment, then strung the bow. Leaning back, she took aim and sent the arrow up into the canopy. It went over the top of a branch and got tangled.

"Now for the hard part." She pulled on the line until the shaft was free, then carefully fed more line and lowered the arrow an inch at a time until it was back on the ground. "All you do is tie your rope onto the fishing line and pull it up over the top of the branch. Of course, it always gets hung up. It took me over four hours to get the first rope set.

After that, it usually goes pretty smoothly. Are you ready?"

"I guess so."

She gave me a hard hat, gloves, and goggles. "You won't need the goggles until we get into the canopy. A lot of people don't use them, but I don't like worrying about my eyes when I'm up there."

I started to pull myself up the rope. She had a special clamping devise that held you in place, while you got your next handhold. It was a lot harder than I expected. I had to pause every few feet to catch my breath. Flanna paused along with me, but it was clear she didn't need to.

The first hundred feet or so there was nothing to see but the vine-covered trunk. This changed dramatically when we passed through the lower story of the canopy. It was a different world—a world that couldn't be seen from below or from up above, flying the Morpho.

The canopy was alive with plants and animals: spiders, scorpions, centipedes, lizards, frogs, snakes, and little, colorful birds. We stopped to look at a three-toed sloth hanging upside down. Its long hair was tinted green and blended perfectly with the moss-covered branch it clung to.

I saw a gigantic spider web with several large shapes wrapped in silk.

"Bats and birds," Flanna said.

What kind of spider eats bats and birds? I thought. "How big is it?"

"You don't want to know."

There were dozens of beautifully colored orchids and other plants I couldn't identify.

"Most of these plants are different types of lichens and bromeliads. They're air plants," Flanna said. "There's no soil up here. They get their nutrients from small particles of dust dissolved in rain."

She went on to explain that some types of bromeliads have leaves that overlap, forming bowls that store water.

"Like this one." She carefully parted the leaves of a large plant. At the base was a little pool of water, and sitting in the middle of the pool was a bright red frog no bigger than my thumb. "Poison arrow frog. It's called that because it secretes a toxin that some tribes distill and put on the end of darts and arrows. The frog's bright color warns potential predators that they're in for a surprise if they try to make a snack out of it."

A little further on, I saw a fierce-looking insect about an inch long, covered in what looked like body armor.

"It's called a paraponera ant. It's also known as a bullet ant, because that's what it feels like when it stings you."

It was bigger than any ant I'd ever seen. It looked like a little tank.

"Listen," Flanna said. She broke off a long twig and poked the ant. It spun around with its large jaws wide open and let out a threatening screech. The noise was exactly what Scarlet would sound like if she were only an inch long.

We finally reached the branch that the ropes were tied to. "We'll rest here."

The branch was three feet around and covered with a virtual garden of large-leafed plants, orchids, bromeliads, and ants! As soon as I sat down, the ants started snapping at me. I scooted further down the branch to get out of their way and came to a carpet of thick moss that continued up the trunk of the tree. After checking to make sure there wasn't anything hiding in it that would bite me, I leaned back. It was as comfortable as an easy chair.

I looked up. About thirty feet above me were several ropes leading off in different directions.

"That's my web," Flanna said. "That's how I get around from tree to tree."

Now that I was sitting, I could feel the tree swaying back and forth. It was a little unnerving.

"You'll get used to the motion in a minute," Flanna said. "It's like being on the deck of a boat. You just have to learn to move with it."

"As long as you don't fall out," I said.

"Yeah, that can hurt."

"What kind of tree is this?"

"Brazil nut. Are you hungry?"

Without waiting for an answer, Flanna stood up on her toes as casually as if she were standing on a city sidewalk. She reached to the next branch and pulled off a pod about the size of a soccer ball. She set it down in front of me and sliced it open with one swing from her machete. Inside were twenty or thirty of the most delicious Brazil nuts I had ever tasted.

There was a sudden motion above us, and Scarlet landed on the branch.

Flanna didn't act surprised. "She always seems to show up when I have food."

"I thought Scarlet hated you."

"Not anymore." She gave Scarlet a Brazil nut. "She drops by every day. Her friends are still a little shy." She pointed up.

The flock was about fifty feet above us.

Flanna explained that despite the heavy rainfall in the Amazon Basin, three quarters of the yearly precipitation comes from the moisture released into the air by the plants.

"If enough trees are removed, the precipitation cycle will be broken, and the result will be extended dry periods that will kill the canopy and the animals that live here."

I realized that the jaguars were only a small part of why the rain forest needed to be preserved. The important part was here in the canopy, where, Flanna said, three quarters of the forest animals lived—many of them never touching the ground.

I also realized that Flanna was as committed to her work in the treetops as Doc was to his work on the ground.

"Now that I have you captive," Flanna said, "perhaps we should talk about your maniac father and me."

I liked Flanna, but I didn't know if I was ready to talk about this with her.

"If you're uncomfortable, we don't have to. . . ."

"No," I said. "Go ahead." But it did seem a little odd, sitting up in a tree talking about my father with his girlfriend.

"I guess one thing you should know is that if you and he go back to Poughkeepsie, I'd like to go with you," Flanna said.

"What about your work down here?"

"It might be nice to go back to the States for a while."

"Sounds like you and Doc have talked about this."

"A little," she said. "He's determined to go back so you can go to school."

This was bad news. I thought that he would change his mind once he got into the project.

"I don't know what the big deal is," I said. "You both have Ph.D.'s. Why can't you teach me what I need to know?"

Flanna laughed. "I used the same argument on him."

"And?"

"And he said no."

"Pigheaded!"

"Exactly! But don't give up hope. If we both keep working on him, maybe we can get him to change his mind."

"That would be a first," I said. "But I'm glad to know you're on my side."

Flanna smiled.

"Are you ready to go higher?"

* * *

I spent the rest of the afternoon with her. We crossed over to three different trees. To accomplish this, we hung upside down and pulled ourselves along the outstretched ropes. The only thing stopping us from a 150-foot drop was a small, stainless-steel pulley.

Just as I was about to climb down and go back to camp, the wind picked up and thick dark clouds moved in over the canopy.

"Looks like the afternoon flight is scratched," I said.

"I was kind of hoping this wouldn't happen your first time up," Flanna said.

"A little storm isn't going to bother me."

Flanna raised her eyebrows. "We better find a good place to ride this out."

We climbed up to one of her observation platforms, which were pretty luxurious. They were made out of plywood covered with thick foam rubber for comfort, and plastic to keep the foam rubber dry. A waterproof tarp hung over the top and mosquito netting was draped around the sides to keep the insects out.

"The platforms are designed for long stays," Flanna said, as we climbed in. "I once spent three weeks on a platform. After a while I felt like I had been transformed into a bromeliad. I just lay there and watched the canopy life pass in front of me. It was the most wonderful experience I've ever had."

The rain started to fall in huge, cold drops. It felt and sounded as if we were sitting under a glacial waterfall, but the worst was yet to come. The wind started gusting through the canopy, and the tree began whipping back and forth like a telephone line in a hurricane. I was sure that it was going to snap in two at any moment.

Fortunately, the storm passed as quickly as it had come. When it was over, I couldn't tell whether I was shivering from the cold rain or from terror.

"That wasn't as bad as I thought it would be," Flanna commented.

I realized something else that day. Flanna was the toughest human I had ever met in my entire life. She and Doc were perfect for each other.

Chapter 18

I took off in the Morpho early the next morning, eager to find out if Beth had wandered farther away. Before checking her, though, I flew to the east and checked on Wild Bill and Taw. They were both in the same areas as the day before. I quickly went through frequencies of the other animals Doc had collared. The paca's signal was in almost the same location as Wild Bill's. If the signal was in the same spot during the afternoon flight, it could mean that Wild Bill had gotten a little fresh paca for breakfast.

I flew back over the lake to the west and picked up Beth's signal almost immediately. She hadn't moved very far, which was good news. But it still didn't explain why she had left her cubs. Perhaps it was just time for her to move on with her life, and time for them to move on with theirs.

It was such a beautiful morning! The clear sky was almost

turquoise, and the canopy was bright green without a spot of mist hanging over it. Somewhere below, Doc and Raul were wandering around looking for jaguars. I hoped Doc was taking it easy, but I kind of doubted it.

I decided to do a little exploring of my own and continued flying west. The canopy stretched below me like a green ocean. I flew in a straight line for ten minutes, then banked to the right and started back to the lake. As I completed my turn, I saw something I hadn't seen on the way out. It was a small hill or a mound, slightly higher than the surrounding canopy. If the light hadn't been just right, I would have missed it completely. I didn't know if it was unusual enough for Silver, but it was the only odd formation I'd seen so far. I flew over the top and got the coordinates with the GPS.

When I got back to the lake, Silver was in camp drinking a cup of coffee. He looked well rested and I knew it wouldn't be too long before he took off again for one of his strolls. I told him about the mound and gave him the information from the GPS. He wanted to know how tall the mound was, how big around it was, and what it was covered with.

"I don't know," I said. "It was sort of a little hill covered with trees. I almost missed it."

"Well, maybe I'll go check it out."

"What are you looking for, Silver?"

"Nothing, really," he said, innocently. "I'm just trying to

keep busy while we're here. Not much for a landlocked skipper to do."

"You could help Doc," I suggested.

"I think Raul is doing just fine in that department."

He was probably right. I got my towel and went up to the rock.

And that's when I found the golden jaguar. It was in exactly the same spot where I had left the pencil. The figurine was small, about the size of my thumb, but very heavy. The jaguar was crouching, as if it were about to pounce on something. Tiny rosettes dotted its golden body.

At first I wondered if I had missed it the day before. But I knew I hadn't. I couldn't possibly have overlooked something like this. My second thought was that it wasn't really made out of gold and that Silver had put it there as some kind of a joke. But Silver wasn't a practical joker. Perhaps Doc and Raul had come back while I was out flying. But where did Raul get something like this? If it was made out of gold, it was worth a lot of money.

I walked back to camp. Silver was still there, drinking another cup of coffee. I heard Flanna rummaging around inside her and Doc's tent.

"Have you seen Doc and Raul?"

"I thought you said they were out looking for jaguars," Silver said.

"I was just wondering if they got back while I was up in the Morpho."

Jaguar

Flanna came out of her tent. I asked her if she had seen them.

"No," she said. "What makes you think they're back?"

"Nothing," I said. "I was just wondering."

I walked back down to the water. Silver followed me.

"What's going on, Jake?"

"I'm not sure."

"Something on your mind?"

I nodded and opened my hand, showing him the jaguar. When he picked it up, his hand trembled slightly.

"Where did you get this?"

I pointed to the rock and explained how Raul and I had been leaving gifts for each other.

"Raul didn't leave you this." He looked around the perimeter of the lake. "And he didn't leave you the other things. I should have known!"

"What are you talking about?"

"We're not alone."

"What do you mean?"

"There must be an uncontacted tribe in the area. A small band of Indians that nobody knows about. Isolated for years."

"Wow!"

"This is a very bad situation, Jake."

"Why?"

He raised his voice. "Because they're very unpredictable, that's why."

"But the gifts," I said. "Why would they—"

"No more gifts! In fact, I don't want you to go up to the rock anymore. Just stay away from it. It will only encourage them. Maybe we'll get lucky and they'll leave us alone."

"What about Doc and Raul?"

"What about them?"

"Are they in any danger?"

Silver thought about this for a few moments. "I don't think so, but we'll all have to be more careful from now on."

"I better tell Flanna," I said, turning to go.

"Wait."

I thought Silver was going to tell me not to, but instead he followed me up to camp.

I went over the story again and showed the jaguar to Flanna. She agreed with Silver that I shouldn't go up to the rock anymore.

"I want you to carry a gun," Silver said to her.

"Forget it, Silver! I agree that we should discourage contact, but that doesn't include shooting at them. So far, they've done nothing wrong. We're the ones that don't belong here."

"What does that mean?"

"We're the worst thing that could ever happen to these people. As soon as Bob and Raul get back, we should leave."

"I think you're overreacting," Silver said. "This site is perfect. Why should we leave?"

"It *was* perfect. And I'm not overreacting. You know as well as I do what happens when we come in contact with these people. We win. They lose."

Flanna walked off into the rain forest, leaving Silver standing there shaking his head.

"Now that's an opinionated woman," he said.

I thought about the Indians I had seen in Manaus and at the camp in the mining town. Flanna was right. Nothing good could come from our having further contact with them.

"I'd like to see the other things they left," Silver said.

I went into my tent and brought out the small box I was using to keep the gifts in. He picked up each one and looked at it closely.

"Mind if I borrow these things?" he asked. "I have some old books back in my cabin. I might come across something in one of them that describes gifts like these."

That seemed very unlikely, but I told Silver I didn't mind. I put the golden jaguar in the box and gave it to him.

CHAPTER 19

Two days passed and still no sign of Doc and Raul. Flanna and I were very worried about them. Silver said that our anxiety was a result of our knowing that we weren't alone. I'm sure this was part of it, at least for me. I'd look around at the thick forest cover and wonder if someone was watching us. What did he think of us? Had he left another gift on the rock? Was he wondering why I hadn't taken it and left something in exchange? I had to stop myself from checking the rock a dozen times a day.

The other part of our anxiety was Doc's rundown condition when he left camp. He had said they would be back in a few days. In Doc's warped sense of time, this could mean anything from a week to several weeks. The only thing that brought us comfort was the fact that Raul was with him.

So we waited. Silver stayed close to camp, but he didn't talk to us much. I carried the shotgun when he was around but stashed it when I was with Flanna, because I knew it made her uncomfortable.

I continued to make my telemetry flights. Wild Bill and Taw had moved, but they were still east of the lake. Beth had stayed within a five-mile radius west of the lake. The hunting must have been good there.

When I wasn't flying, I helped Flanna in the canopy. She was serious about leaving as soon as Doc got back. We had taken down most of her web, leaving only two research platforms.

We talked a lot about what had happened to Brazil's indigenous peoples. Millions had been killed over the years—entire tribes wiped out by rain forest exploitation. She said the most effective means of getting rid of them had been to go into their villages and cough on them.

"For them a flu virus, or measles, can be as bad as the bubonic plague or AIDS," she told me. "The diseases of civilization are the same bullets that killed hundreds of thousands of North American Indians. Down here, those that survive the diseases are contaminated by Western civilization. They work in the mines and oil fields for a few pennies a day and the privilege of living in total squalor."

On the morning of the third day, Doc returned.

Flanna and I were up in the canopy. I was lying face down on one of the observation platforms, looking through the foliage, when I caught a slight movement on the ground below. I found the binoculars and shifted over to the right

of the platform so I'd have a clearer view. All I could see was
a pair of muddy boots lying on the ground. The wind moved
the branch I was trying to see around, and I got a glimpse
of a pair of torn Levi's blue jeans.

"It's Doc!" I yelled, scrambling for my rope.

By the time I reached the ground Flanna was already
there and out of her harness. She was cradling Doc's head
in her lap. His eyes were closed and his lips were swollen
and cracked. He was having trouble breathing.

"We have to get him back to camp," Flanna said. "He's
burning up."

I ran. When I got to camp, I yelled for Silver, but he
didn't answer. I didn't wait around to find out why. I
grabbed the jaguar stretcher and ran back into the forest.

* * *

Flanna thought Doc had malaria, but she wasn't certain. She
said it wasn't the first time, which was news to me.

"It could be a flare-up," she said. "Stress can bring it out
again. Or else he hasn't been taking his antimalaria pills and
he's been infected."

That wouldn't surprise me.

Whatever he had was very serious. We put him on a cot
in his tent. He had a raging fever and was nearly comatose.
Flanna dribbled water into his mouth and sponged him
down, trying to cool him off. She force fed him a huge dose
of antimalaria pills.

"This won't work unless it's malaria," she said. "I guess all we can do is try to keep him comfortable and hope the fever breaks."

I wandered in and out of the tent all afternoon and evening, bringing water up from the lake to cool Doc down. We hadn't seen Silver all day. He couldn't have picked a worse time to go out for one of his strolls.

That night I came back from the lake with yet another load of water. When I got to the tent, Flanna was in tears.

"I don't know what to do, Jake. I think he's getting worse!"

The man lying on the cot did not look like my father. In the dim lantern light he looked like the ghost of Robert Lansa. It took all my strength to hold back my own tears. My father couldn't die like this.

Flanna wiped her tears away. "No sign of Silver yet?"

I shook my head. I thought he'd be back by evening, but he hadn't shown up. Nor had Raul. What had happened to them out there? Raul wouldn't leave Doc like this.

"There's nothing we can do for him here," Flanna said. "He needs medical attention. We have to get him to a doctor."

"How?"

"The boat," she said.

"What about Silver and Raul?"

"We'll come back for them."

A trip down the tunnel right now would probably kill Doc.

"Who would pilot the boat?" I asked. "I don't know how

to do it. If we ran aground in the tunnel, all of us would die, including Silver and Raul. The boat's our only way out of here."

"You're right," she said. "But we need to do something."

I had never felt more helpless.

"Do you want me to take over?" I asked. She hadn't left Doc's side in twelve hours.

"No. I'm fine," she said. "I just wish Silver would get back here!"

"I'm sure he'll be back tonight or tomorrow morning," I said, but I wasn't at all certain. Something might have happened to him, too.

I left the tent and walked down to the beach. I was hoping to see a light on in Silver's boat, but it was dark and the Zodiac was still on the beach. The moon was full, and I could see the *Tito* clearly bobbing near the tunnel's entrance.

I sat down and thought about ways to help my father. In the morning I could try to find Silver. But where would I start looking? I couldn't track him the way Raul could.

Maybe the tribe could help us, I thought. They might know what Doc's problem was. Then again, they might be responsible for his problem and Raul's disappearance.

I began to wonder if there really was an uncontacted tribe. Raul wasn't with Doc, which meant that he could have left the golden jaguar. That still didn't explain where he had gotten the figurine.

I glanced over to the rock. I could see it clearly in the

moonlight. What if there was another gift up there? Perhaps it would explain what was going on. What would be the harm in just looking?

I climbed up to the rock and turned my flashlight on. In the beam was a rusty pair of eyeglasses. I picked the frames up. The lenses were missing. Raul didn't wear glasses, nor did anyone else in our group. And I doubted that the tribe had an optometrist living with it. Where would they get a pair of glasses? I was even more confused.

I looked out across the lake. The full moon reflected off the surface, and I was reminded of something I had read when I was in Poughkeepsie.

I ran over to the Zodiac, started it up, and sped across the lake to Silver's boat.

His cabin was unlocked. I went inside and switched on the light and found the book I was looking for. It took me awhile to find the right page:

> **A river running through the forest beside the city fell over a big fall whose roar could be heard for leagues, and below the fall the river seemed to widen out into a great lake emptying itself they had no notion where.**

The tunnel, I thought. The lake wasn't "great" and the waterfall couldn't be heard for "leagues," but who knows what kind of changes had taken place here since 1753, when this description was written? The lake the book was talking about was supposed to be near the lost mines of Muribeca.

I looked over at Silver's desk and was surprised to see a radio collar lying on it. What was even more surprising was that the transmitter had been cut away from the collar. Why would he do that?

Sitting next to the collar was my box of gifts. I opened it. Inside was the golden jaguar, various feathers, the turtle skull, the blue stone, the dried piranha jaw, and a new item—an old rusty compass. I picked it up and turned it over. There was an engraving on the back. It read: COLONEL P. H. FAWCETT, 1924.

I knew why Silver wanted to come up here.

I took the Zodiac to shore. Before going in to check on Doc, I went to the supply tent. One of the receivers and handheld antennas was missing.

Silver had cut the radio collar transmitter off and left it on the rock as a gift. Right now he was out in the forest tracking the Indian who had taken it, hoping he would lead him to the place where he had found the golden jaguar.

Colonel Fawcett was a courageous man and a great explorer. But he was chasing after something that never existed. The fruitless search killed him, his son, and his son's friend. It's a tragedy that's as old as the rain forest. . . .

Silver had lied to me. He had lied to all of us.

Flanna was sitting in the chair next to Doc's cot, asleep. I touched her on the shoulder, and she woke up with a start.

"Why don't you go to my tent and rest," I whispered.

"Are you sure?"

"Yeah. I'm wide awake," I said, which wasn't an exaggeration.

"I'll be back soon. Just keep putting the cold compresses on."

"Is he any better?"

"I don't know. He's been talking, but none of it makes sense. Delirious ramblings."

I watched Doc all night. Every once in a while he would start mumbling, as if he were having a nightmare. I couldn't understand what he was saying. About two in the morning he sat straight up in bed and yelled, "Watch out, Beth! You're smarter than that!"

I was so startled I almost fell over backward. As soon as he said it, he lay back down, and didn't say another thing the rest of the night.

CHAPTER 20

Flanna came in just after sunrise. I debated telling her about Silver, but had decided against it. It wouldn't do her any good to know about what he was up to. Right now the important thing was to find him and convince him to take Doc out of here.

"No change," I said.

"Why don't you go rest?"

"Okay," I said, but I had no intention of resting. I walked out of the tent.

During the night I had gotten the frequency of the collar Silver had taken out of Doc's logbook. My plan was to take the Morpho up, mark the signal on the GPS, then go in on foot. The trick would be talking Silver into coming back with me.

I suspected he had been looking for the lost mines of Muribeca for years. This would explain a lot of different things. . . . The books in his library, his eagerness to take us upriver for next to nothing, and his insistence on going through the tunnel.

The most important question was one I didn't like thinking about. Did Silver blow up the boat in Manaus so he could take us upriver? Was he responsible for Bill Brewster's death? If so, what would stop him from killing me when he found out I knew all about his scheme?

I went down to the lake, uncovered the Morpho, and took off. I picked up the signal from the missing collar almost immediately. The Indian was west of the lake near the mound, which I figured must have something to do with the lost mines. I flew over the top of the signal and marked it with the GPS.

I flew straight back to the lake without bothering to check the collared jaguars. They could wait, my father couldn't.

I pulled the Morpho on shore and started to put the tarp over it.

"Nice landing, Ace."

I turned around. A man was standing behind me. He was carrying an automatic rifle and had a scar on his face—although the scar was hard to see in the midst of all the insect bites. I hoped he had enjoyed his trip up the tunnel.

My shotgun was about ten feet away from me.

"Don't." He picked up the shotgun and threw it into the lake.

So much for that idea. "What do you want?" I asked.

He didn't answer. I heard someone coming down the path leading to the camp. It was Fred Stoats from the mining town!

"What's going on in camp?" the man asked him, without taking his eyes off me.

"I didn't see anybody, Tyler," Fred said.

"What do you mean, you didn't see anybody?"

"I'm telling you the truth!" Fred insisted.

"What are you doing up here, Fred?" I asked.

He smiled a toothless grin. "I told you that you should have taken me upriver with you."

"But how——"

"Shut up!" Tyler said, and knocked me down with the butt of his rifle. "Tie him up."

Fred flipped me over and tied my hands behind my back. Tyler pointed his rifle at me. "Where's Colonel Silver?"

Colonel? "He's not here," I said.

"I'm about out of patience."

"You better tell him," Fred said to me.

"He left a couple of days ago and we haven't seen him. I have no idea where he went."

"We'll see about that," Tyler said. "So who's up in camp?"

I didn't see any point in lying about this. "Flanna Brenna and my dad. They're in a tent. That's why he didn't see them. My dad's sick and Flanna is taking care of him."

"We'll see about that, too," Tyler said. "Get on your feet."

I stood up.

"What do you want me to do, Tyler?" Fred asked.

"How about keeping your mouth shut for ten minutes? That would be very helpful."

I had a feeling that Tyler wasn't exactly fond of Fred Stoats.

"We're going to walk up to your camp very quietly," Tyler said. "When we get there, I want you to call them. If you pull any crap, I'll pull this trigger and that'll be all she wrote. Do you understand the plan?"

I nodded. I could hear my heart beating in my chest.

"Good. Let's go."

When we got there, Tyler had me drop to my knees. He put the barrel of his gun against my head.

"Okay, call them out."

"Flanna?" I said. My mouth was so dry I could barely speak.

"Louder." He bumped my head with the barrel.

"Flanna!"

She came right out and froze when she saw me. "What——"

"Just come on over here, honey, and join the party. Or I'm going to make a real mess of this boy's head."

Flanna walked over to me very slowly, and Tyler motioned for her to join me on the ground. Fred tied her hands behind her back.

"You're the man from the hospital," she said.

"You know him?" I asked in shock.

"He's one of the men who offered to take us upriver after the accident."

"Shut up!" Tyler shouted, pointing the rifle at her. He looked at the tent. "Dr. Lansa!"

"He's sick," Flanna said. "He can't even walk!"

"Fred, go over and take a look."

Fred went into the tent and came right back out. "She's telling the truth. He looks real bad."

"Are there any weapons in there?"

Fred went back inside and came out shaking his head. "The tent's clean."

Tyler pointed the rifle at me. "Where's the Indian?"

"What Indian?"

"Don't get cute. The one who helped you catch that jaguar downriver."

"He didn't come up here with us."

"I believe that's the first truthful thing you've said today, boy. An Indian with a bucketful of money would have much better sense than to come up here. Fred, go search the other tents."

"What's this all about?" Flanna asked.

"My advice for both of you is to just stay quiet for the time being," Tyler said. "I'm very tired."

Fred came back from searching the tents. "Just supplies," he said.

"Go out to Silver's boat and see what you can find."

Tyler didn't say anything else until he heard the Zodiac start up.

"Okay," he said. "I'm going to ask again. Where's Colonel Silver?"

"I already—"

"Not you! Her."

"I don't know," Flanna said. "He left a couple of days ago. We've been waiting for him to come back so we can get out of here."

"Why would you want to get out of here?"

"Because Bob's sick. We need to get him to a doctor."

"And Silver doesn't know he's sick?"

"He got sick after Silver left," I said.

Tyler sat down about ten feet away from us and just looked at us through tired eyes. I didn't know about Flanna, but this really frightened me. Not that I wasn't scared before, but there was something even more menacing about him just sitting there staring at us.

I heard the boat start up and come across the lake. A few minutes later, Fred came back into camp. He had my box of gifts with him.

"What's this?"

"I found it in Silver's cabin."

Tyler flipped the box over on the ground and looked at the contents. The golden jaguar wasn't there. I guess Fred decided not to share that little item. Tyler picked the old compass up and read the back. He smiled.

"Jake, do you have any idea where Colonel Silver found this?"

I shook my head.

"I see." Tyler stood up. "Pick that stuff up, Fred."

As Fred bent down to pick up the gifts, something bright and shiny fell out of his shirt pocket. Uh-oh, Fred. He tried to cover it up with his hand before Tyler saw it, but he was too late.

"Let's see it, Fred."

Fred handed him the figurine. Fred looked as if he was about to throw up.

Tyler looked at the jaguar closely. "I wish you hadn't done that, Fred."

"I was going to show it to you," Fred said. He started to back away.

Tyler shot him in the chest. Fred flew backward, hitting the ground about ten feet away.

Flanna and I just stared.

"As you can see," Tyler said, "I'm a very serious man, and I want some very serious answers. The next person to go will be your father, Jake. Then I'll kill Flanna. Then I'll kill you. Do you understand?"

I nodded.

"Good. Now, tell me where Silver is."

I didn't know what to do. If I didn't tell him how to find Silver, then he might just kill us all and wait for Silver to come back to camp. Of course, he might just kill us, anyway.

*J*aguar

He started walking toward Doc's tent.

"Wait!"

He stopped and turned back around.

"Silver's looking for the lost mines of Muribeca!"

He smiled. "He hasn't found them yet?"

"I don't think so."

Flanna was totally shocked.

"What about this?" He tossed the jaguar up into the air and caught it.

I told him about the gifts, the tribe, and the radio collar.

"The colonel was always a clever one."

"What are you going to do?"

"Well, the first thing I'm going to do is to take a little nap. The colonel is not the kind of man you want to approach when you're tired. It took us three tries to find the right tributary, and I didn't have a nice boat like yours. You can imagine what that was like. And then there was Fred—not the best traveling companion. The only reason I let him go with me was because Silver sabotaged my boat and I needed another. Fred helped me steal one."

"What about us?" Flanna asked.

"For now, I'm going to tie you to separate trees. I can't have you running around while I'm trying to take a nap. And I don't want you putting your heads together and making big plans. Believe me, it's for your own protection."

CHAPTER 21

Tyler crawled into the hammock outside the cook tent and fell asleep with his rifle resting on his chest. Flanna was about fifty feet away from me, tied to another tree. I could see her struggling to get loose, but it didn't do her any good.

Tyler didn't wake until late afternoon. The first thing he did was to check on Doc. When he came out, he looked at Flanna and said, "He's alive, but he doesn't look good."

He went into the cook tent and came back out eating something.

"I guess I'm about ready to move out." He walked over and untied me. "I want you to get the map and show me where that collar is. Then I want you to get the telemetry gear and show me how it works."

I brought out a map and showed him the last telemetry location. Then I brought out a receiver and a collar and showed him how to track with it.

"What's the frequency of the collar I'm after?"

I gave him the number and he dialed it in and held the antenna up. He didn't pick up the signal.

"You're too far away," I said. "You'll have to get within five miles before you pick it up."

He wasn't happy about this. "Any reason why I should trust you?"

"No," I said. "But I could care less what happens to Silver. He set us up!"

Tyler laughed. "That's the spirit."

"Now, what's going to happen to us?"

"I'm going to tie you back up. Then I'm going to find my old friend Silver."

"What about my father?"

"I'm afraid he's on his own."

"We can't just leave him in the tent by himself," Flanna shouted.

"Well, that's exactly what we're going to do," Tyler said.

He tied me to a tree and walked out of camp. I heard the Zodiac start and go across the lake.

"You should have told me about Silver," Flanna said.

"I didn't put it together until last night, but you're right. I should have told you."

I looked over at Doc's tent. There was a movement inside. A moment later, Doc came stumbling outside and fell down.

"Dad!"

"Bob!"

He slowly got to his feet and stood there for a moment trying to get his balance. I heard the Zodiac start back up and come across the lake.

"What's going on?" Doc asked.

"There's no time to explain," Flanna said. "You need to go back into the tent and act as if you're dead."

Doc hesitated.

"Just do what Flanna said!" I shouted.

He turned around and stumbled back inside. A minute later, Tyler came back into camp carrying a backpack slung over his shoulder.

"If Silver happens to show up while I'm gone, tell him that I fixed all the boats just like he fixed mine. If he wants the missing parts, he can come and find me. I got them right here." He patted the pack.

"And Jake, this little tracking thing better work. If it doesn't . . . Well, I'm sure you can put two and two together. Have a good day."

Tyler walked out of camp. Flanna and I just stared at each other. She waited about ten minutes, then yelled to Doc that it was all right to come out. He came out of the tent and walked over to me on shaky legs.

"What's going on?" he asked.

He was in bad shape, and I was afraid he would pass out before he could cut me loose.

"You need to get a knife to cut the ropes," I said very slowly.

He nodded and stumbled over to the cook tent and came back with a knife. Without a word, he cut through my ropes. As soon as I was free, he collapsed. I went over to Flanna and cut her rope. Then we both ran back over to Doc.

"I didn't have time to tell you," she said. "But before that maniac came into camp, your father was showing some signs of improvement." She cradled Doc's head in her lap. "I'm afraid he's relapsed. What's going on, Jake?"

"You know as much as I do. Silver's looking for the Muribeca gold mine, and Tyler's looking for him."

"We need to find a place to hide before Tyler gets back."

"He won't be back for a while."

"As soon as he finds Silver, he'll—"

"He's not going to find him," I told her. "I gave him Beth's radio frequency, not the Indian's. She'll hear Tyler coming a mile away. He'll never get close to her."

"But he'll be back eventually."

"Hopefully I'll be able to find Silver before Tyler returns." I tried to sound confident.

"What do you mean?"

"I'm going to go out and look for him."

"I don't think that's a good idea, Jake."

"Why not?"

"What if Silver doesn't want to help us? He's up to his neck in this. There's no telling what he'll do."

I hadn't quite worked through this part of the plan, but I didn't want to debate it with her. There wasn't enough time. Finding Silver was our only hope.

"Maybe we should get Doc back into the tent," I said. "We can talk about this later."

"You're right."

We carried him back into the tent.

"I'll go down and get more water," I said.

I ran to the lake and got into the Zodiac. Tyler had taken the spark plug out of the engine, so I had to paddle out to the boat. I found Silver's underwater flashlight, a box of shotgun shells, and some dry rags. I wanted to try to find the shotgun Tyler had thrown into the lake. If he returned while I was gone, I hoped Flanna would have a change of heart about using it.

I got back into the Zodiac and paddled out to where I thought Tyler had tossed the shotgun. I stripped my clothes off and dove in. The bottom was deeper than I expected. I also had thought that it would be flat and sandy in the middle, as it was alongshore, but instead it was covered with huge blocky stones. I ran out of breath and had to come back up for air.

I dove again. Just as I reached the bottom, something very large came at me from behind one of the stones. A dolphin! I was so startled I nearly sucked in a lungful of water. The dolphin passed within inches of me and disappeared into the gloom.

Jaguar

I shone my flashlight in the dolphin's wake and saw something glittering in the light. I knew it wasn't the shotgun, but I grabbed it anyway, then swam to the surface for air.

I held onto the side of the Zodiac with my left hand and caught my breath. I opened my right hand and stared in amazement. It was another golden jaguar, about three times the size of the first one. I realized that the stones beneath the lake might not be just big rocks but the ruins of a city—perhaps the fabled lost city connected with the Muribeca gold mines. The rest of the city was probably all around us, buried under centuries of tropical decomposition. Silver didn't have to look further than our own backyard for his precious treasure.

There was no time to celebrate my discovery. We still needed to get Doc out of here, and our only hope of achieving this was being stalked by a psychopath. I had to find Silver before Tyler did.

I dove again without success. I resurfaced and looked up at the sky. Dark, ugly clouds were starting to move in, and the trees around the lake were beginning to sway.

One more dive, I told myself. I saw the dolphin again, but it kept its distance. I searched until my lungs felt as if they were going to burst. Then I saw the shotgun. It was lying at the bottom near a particularly large stone. I grabbed the gun and swam back to the surface.

I climbed into the Zodiac and paddled to shore. When I got there, I took the shotgun apart and dried it off with the rags. When I finished, I ran back to camp.

Flanna was in the tent with Doc. Quietly, I put the shotgun and box of shells outside the entrance, then went inside with the bucket of water.

"How is he?"

"Not good." She dipped a cloth into the bucket and started sponging him down.

I slipped back outside and went over to the tent where we had our gear stored and grabbed two bundles of climbing rope. I hoped it was enough to do the trick.

I ran back down to the lake, started the Morpho, and took off. Before I left the area, I flew over camp and waggled my wings. Flanna came out of the tent to see what was going on. Wish me luck, Flanna, I thought, and I headed west.

CHAPTER 22

When I got to a thousand feet above the canopy, I leveled off. The wind was really blowing, and I had to fight the stick all the way. This was not the best weather to be flying in. My only consolation was that I wouldn't be flying for long.

I picked up the signal and flew until I was right over the top of it. Here we go, I thought. I switched the engine off.

It got very, very quiet. I pushed the nose forward into a dive. When the altimeter reached two hundred feet, I flipped the red switch. There was a loud *pop* and, a second later, a hard upward jerk as the parachute filled with air. I braced myself as I floated down to the canopy. Sorry, Buzz.

The initial impact wasn't as bad as I had expected. The Morpho settled onto the top of the canopy and hesitated there for a moment. There was a loud cracking sound, and I dropped about twenty feet, then came to a bone-wrenching stop. I breathed a deep sigh of relief. So far so good.

I looked around for a branch that I could get a rope around, but it was hard to see in the dim light. There was a gust of wind and I was suddenly jerked upward. The wind had filled the parachute again! The left wing smashed into a branch and bent like a piece of baling wire. Then the right wing crumpled. I looked down. I was swinging freely about 150 feet above the ground. My only hope of getting out of this alive was to swing over and try to get ahold of one of the vines running up a tree trunk. I tied my two ropes together and let one end drop. The Morpho slipped another ten feet, then caught again. This was probably the dumbest thing I had ever done.

I started to swing the Morpho back and forth. I reached out for the nearest vine, but missed it by a good five feet. Two more swings, I thought, and my momentum will get me close enough to grab it. My next grab was closer, but not close enough. I knew I wasn't going to be able to reach the vine on the next pass unless I took off my safety belt and leaned out. I quickly tied the rope around my wrist, unsnapped my belt, and squatted with my legs on the seat. I waited until the very last second. Then, just as the Morpho reached the end of its swing, I lunged for the trunk.

I clung to the vines with all my strength. I heard a loud tearing sound and turned my head. The Morpho dropped from sight. Now all I had to do was to get to the ground, which seemed relatively easy compared to what I had just been through.

There was a loud screeching noise, and Scarlet grabbed onto the trunk about two inches from my face. I nearly fell out of the tree.

"What are you doing here?" I shouted.

Her eyes dilated and the featherless area around her beak turned bright pink. All I needed now was to have an enraged macaw tear my ear off.

"It's okay, Scarlet," I said quietly, trying to calm her down. "We'll be fine."

Either she had followed the Morpho, or Silver wasn't far away. She screeched again and flew off. I was happy to see her go.

I tied the rope around the thickest vine I could reach and tested it by jerking on it. I let myself down the rope very slowly, making sure I always had something to grab onto in case the vine didn't hold.

At one point I grabbed a thick glob of spider web and pulled my hand away as if I had stuck it into a fire. I'm not fond of spiders—especially big spiders that eat bats and birds. Fortunately, I didn't disturb the spider or even see it. If I had, I probably would have had a heart attack.

When my feet finally touched the ground, I collapsed and nearly wept with gratitude. I closed my eyes. When I opened them, Silver was standing right in front of me, with Scarlet perched on his shoulder.

"That was quite an entrance," he said.

I looked up at him and didn't say anything.

He looked at the rope. "I take it that the canopy landing wasn't an accident."

At least I wouldn't have to go looking for him, I thought. I felt a mixture of relief and hatred.

"What are you doing here, Jake?"

I stood up. My legs were shaking so badly I had to hold onto the tree to steady myself. "What are *you* doing here?"

"I heard the ultralight's engine cut out and I knew there was a problem."

"That's not what I meant!" I shouted. "You're out here looking for the lost mines of Muribeca. That's why you offered to take us upriver. That's why you insisted on going through the tunnel. That's why you told me not to leave any more gifts on the rock. I know about the transmitter you left."

He looked at me calmly. "You've summed that up nicely," he said. "Now, tell me why you're out here."

"Doc's sick and he needs help."

"What happened?" He looked genuinely concerned.

I told him how Doc had come stumbling back into camp alone. "If you weren't out here looking for that stupid mine, we could have been through the tunnel by now."

Silver frowned and shook his head. "There's no way I could have known, Jake. I'm sorry."

This threw me off a little. He seemed sincere.

"And now your friend Tyler is here," I said.

He tensed. "Where?"

"On a wild jaguar chase with Beth. At least I hope that's where he is. He thinks he's tracking you."

"I need to know everything Tyler said, everything he did."

When I finished explaining, he sat down and leaned against the tree. Suddenly he looked very tired. "Tyler's wanted in almost every country south of the Mexican border, including Brazil. You're lucky he didn't kill you."

"I think he was going to get around to it."

"No doubt."

Silver went on to explain that he and Tyler had been in Vietnam together. When the war ended, he talked Tyler into coming to Brazil to look for the lost mines of Muribeca.

"We followed Fawcett's supposed journey into the Matto Grosso. To fund our expeditions, we hired ourselves out to the highest bidder. Some of the bidders were pretty unpleasant people."

"You were mercenaries?" I said.

"Hired guns," he said, sadly. "It took ten years for us to realize that Matto Grosso was a dead end. Tyler got fed up with the search and found a different way of finding gold. He got into drug running and gun smuggling. We parted ways. I moved to Ecuador, met Alicia, and we had Tito. I was never going to look for the mine again, but then my family disappeared. I bought a boat and spent years looking for them. I finally gave up, and after a while, I started looking for the mines again. I had nothing else to do.

"I figured out that the mines and the lost city were somewhere around here, but I didn't have the money or the permit to get into this area.

"Then Bill and your father showed up. I offered my services, but they turned me down and got their own boat. Tyler found out that I had new information about the mines. He came to Manaus and said he wanted in. I insisted that there was no new information, but of course he didn't buy that story.

"He was desperate . . . on the run, no money. I told him that I didn't have the cash for an expedition or the permit to go into this area and explore. I made a mistake and told him about Bill's permit. The next thing I know the boat blows up."

"He blew the boat up?"

"I'm not sure. But he's an expert at that sort of thing. It would have been easy for him. I think his plan was to steal a boat and offer to take you upriver, which is why I approached your father so soon after Bill's death. Tyler can be very charming when he needs to be."

That wasn't the Tyler I knew.

"So he followed us," I said.

"No, he went ahead of us. When he broke into the cabin, he found a map. There were four different tributaries marked as possible routes to the lake. He waited in the mining town, and I think his plan was to follow us to the right tributary. While you were out catching your jaguar, I found his stolen boat and wrecked his engine. After a week at the lake, I thought we were safe."

"So you knew he was in town all along?"

"I'm afraid so, Jake."

I told him about Tyler and Fred's false starts up the other tributaries.

"That explains the delay," he said.

"You picked a bad time to leave camp."

He nodded. "I knew Flanna wanted to get out of here because of the tribe. I wasn't about to leave without finding out if the Muribeca mines were here. I had to go before Doc came back."

"Did you find the mines?"

"I did. And you're the one that pointed me in the right direction. The Muribeca mines are in the mound you saw from the air."

"What are you going to do about it?"

"Nothing."

I was shocked. This isn't what I had expected.

"I've been thinking a lot the last few weeks," he said. "Mostly about my son, Tito, and the whole problem down here with the Indians. What if he was living in the rain forest like these people are—happy, content with his life? Then some greedy jerk like me comes along and takes it all away from him. It's not right, and I'm ashamed to admit that this thought never entered my mind before I met you and Doc and Flanna. I know where the gold is and that's going to have to be enough."

"How long will it be 'enough?' " I asked.

"Hopefully, for the rest of my life," he said. "I think I'm cured."

I hoped he was right.

"Our big problem now is Tyler," Silver continued.

"I think we should just leave him here," I said.

"Unfortunately, we can't do that. He's an expert in jungle survival. Eventually, he'll stumble onto the tribe and kill them one by one until he gets what he wants. He's done this kind of work in the past for oil and mining companies that found the indigenous population incompatible with their plans. It's one of the many things he's wanted for. I can't let that happen."

"You're going to kill him?"

"Not unless I have to," he said.

"Then . . ."

"I'll try to catch him and turn him over to the authorities."

"What's going to stop him from telling everyone about Muribeca?"

"His greed will stop him. Tyler's not stupid. One way or another he'll get out of prison and come back here. He won't tell anyone about this place until he's gotten his share. If and when he gets out, I'll be waiting for him. Now, at that point I might have to kill him." He smiled. "My new mission is to make sure that the Muribeca mines remain a myth. I was thinking that your dad might want to hire me to be the security force for the preserve."

"If he lives, I'll put a word in for you. What are we going to do now?"

"We have three problems to take care of. Your dad, Tyler, and our friend Raul."

"Raul?"

"I know where he is. In fact, I saw him about two hours ago. He's been captured by our uncontacted friends. He's not hurt and he doesn't look terribly upset about his situation, but we can't just leave him here. I don't know what their plans are for him. When you crashed through the canopy, I was waiting for it to get dark, so I could cut him loose."

Chapter 23

The tribe's encampment was well hidden in a small clearing. By the time we got there, it was almost dark. There was a single, horseshoe shaped structure made out of poles and covered with dry leaves. The roof was shaped like a dome and quite tall. There were several separate compartments facing the center of the horseshoe, with small cooking fires burning outside them. Raul was sitting down, facing one of the poles.

We were about a hundred yards away, hiding under a fallen tree. Scarlet sat on the tree preening herself.

"What if Scarlet screams?" I asked.

"Scarlet and I have been together a long time," Silver said. "She knows when to be quiet."

He set up a small tripod and a spotting scope. I looked through it. Raul's hands and feet were tied around the pole with vines. Silver was right about him not being too upset about his situation. A woman came over to him and started feeding him out of a large gourd. He was smiling and gulping down the food like a baby bird.

"Are you sure we should free him?" I whispered.

"I told you he didn't seem too upset." Silver smiled. "That's the same woman who was feeding him this afternoon. I think we should at least get him out of there and ask him what happened and what he wants to do.

"The problem's going to be getting in there without disturbing them," Silver continued. "I don't want to get into a 'situation'—someone might get hurt in the process."

"So what are we going to do?" I asked.

"I thought I'd wait until they were all asleep, sneak in, and cut him loose. I don't know what else to do."

"Let me go in," I said.

"I don't think . . ."

"I can do it!" I told Silver about how I had learned to stalk in Kenya.

He listened patiently. "That's quite a story, but—"

"If you get caught, we're dead. You're the only one that can get us out of here. I can do this, Silver."

He gave in. "I hope you're right."

We waited and watched. Silver said there were only about twenty of them.

"Four or five of them are little kids, and there are two babies. There might have been a lot more of them at one time. They could be the few survivors of the lost city, which is around here somewhere, or they might be just a tribe that wandered into the area one day and stayed."

I was tempted to tell him about the ruins under the lake, but I held back.

"So Fawcett was here?"

"You saw the compass?"

I nodded.

"He was here all right. He either lied in his letters to his wife about being in Matto Grosso, or he came up here after he was supposed to have disappeared. I don't know if he and his son and their friend were killed here, or whether they decided to stay. He found it, and that might have been enough for him."

I told him about the glasses.

"In the photos I've seen of Fawcett, he never had glasses on. Maybe they belonged to his son, or his son's friend."

After it got dark, it became difficult to pick out details in the village. All we could do was look for movement. We continued to wait. I thought about Doc and wondered how he was doing. I would have given almost anything to be going down the tunnel right now, but we couldn't leave Raul and we still had to do something about Tyler. If we survived, I would have a heck of a dispatch to send back to the Home.

"You about ready?" Silver whispered.

I nodded and started to take my clothes off.

"What are you doing?"

"This is how I do it." I finished undressing and started smearing dirt all over my body.

"What if you step on a snake?"

"I won't."

He handed me his knife, and I started toward the encampment.

When I got to the open end of the horseshoe, I slowed way down. I could hear people snoring. A child coughed and I froze in midstep. My biggest fear was having Raul cry out when I got to him. I had a plan for that, and I hoped it would work.

Raul was slumped over, sleeping. His forehead was resting against the pole. When I got to him, I reached toward his head very, very slowly, then clamped my hand over his mouth. He jerked awake and made a muffled sound that I was sure they would hear. When Raul recognized me, he relaxed. There was some movement in the hammocks, and I held my breath. I sat perfectly still for about five minutes. When it was clear that no one was going to get up, I quietly sliced through the vines around Raul's feet and wrists. He followed me step for step out of the compound.

"Impressive," Silver said, when we got back.

I put my clothes back on, while Raul and he whispered to each other in Portuguese.

"We have a problem," Silver said. "It seems that our friends down there have your female jaguar's collar."

"How did they get that?"

"Your father and Raul stumbled across a jaguar pit when they were out poking around. Apparently the tribe set it for her and she fell right into it. She's dead."

Jaguar

In his delirium, Doc had been calling out the jaguar's name, not my mom's!

"They were on their way back when your father collapsed. Raul left him in the forest and was on his way to camp to get help, when he got caught by the tribe. They hauled him to the village, and he couldn't make them understand that your dad needed help. Raul assumed that Doc had died in the forest. It's a miracle that he made it back to camp."

"So Tyler is heading right toward the village?"

"Right," Silver said. "I figure our best chance is to go out and try to intercept him before he gets here. At least we know where he's headed. Unfortunately, we don't know which direction he'll be coming from."

I thought about this for a minute. "So there's a pit not too far from here?"

"Yeah," Silver said. "But what's that have to do with anything?"

"Does Raul know where the collar is?"

Silver asked him. "He says that it's hanging from one of the beams on the right side of the compound. What do you have in mind?"

"Let me see if I can get the collar first."

Silver and Raul spoke again.

"Raul says his bag is hanging next to the collar. He'd like to have it back if you can manage it."

"I'll see what I can do."

I took my clothes off again.

CHAPTER 24

I had no problem retrieving the collar. It was hanging right where Raul said it would be, alongside Beth's drying skin and Raul's cotton bag. I hoped Wild Bill and Taw would fare better than their mother had in the new preserve.

It was still dark when we got to the jaguar pit, so we rested until daylight. The pit was about ten feet square. There were sharpened branches embedded in the bottom. I lowered myself down with a rope and took the branches out along with the other sticks and leaves that had fallen in when Beth fell through.

When I climbed back out, Raul wanted to know how much Tyler weighed and how much gear he was carrying. I gave him my best guess.

We went to work. Raul kept undoing everything we did. Finally, Silver and I backed off and let Raul do it by himself. He worked quickly, but it was still taking longer than Silver wanted.

Raul laid heavier sticks around the edges of the pit and light sticks in the middle. I guessed this was to make sure that the animal, or in this case the maniac, would be in the middle when the top collapsed.

Raul made a few final touches to the ground around the pit and announced that it was ready.

We hid ourselves fifty feet away. About twenty minutes later, Tyler showed up. He had the earphones on and the receiver strapped to his belt. He held the antenna above his head, and turned it back and forth very slowly, trying to locate where the signal was coming from. The collar was hanging in a tree in back of the pit. At this range he wouldn't be able to locate where the signal was coming from. All he would know was that it was very close.

Without hesitating, Tyler stepped onto the top of the pit. I expected it to collapse, but it didn't. He continued walking and still it didn't cave in.

Raul made an odd sound. Tyler froze when he heard it. Then the ground gave way and he disappeared. We stayed in our hiding place. Silver waited for the dust to settle before he said anything.

"Tyler?" he shouted.

"I should have known!" Tyler shouted back.

"I'm going to toss you a rope," Silver continued. "I want you to climb out very slowly. When you get out of the pit, I want you to keep both your hands on the rope and just follow it until I tell you to stop. If you take one hand off the rope, I'll blow you back into the pit. Understand?"

"Yes, sir," Tyler said.

J a g u a r

Silver threw the rope into the pit. The other end was tied to a tree in back of where we were taking cover.

"Nice and easy."

"I'm coming out." Tyler's head appeared above the edge.

"Just follow the rope," Silver said.

When Tyler was well away from the pit, Silver told him to stop. He said something to Raul in Portuguese. Raul reached into his bag and pulled out some rope.

"One hand at a time, Tyler. You know the routine."

Tyler put one of his hands behind his back. Raul put a loop around it and waited for Tyler's other hand. The second hand shot back like a bolt of lightning and grabbed Raul before any of us knew what was happening. There wasn't time for Silver to get a shot off before Raul and Tyler were tangled up on the ground. Silver fired into the air and Scarlet flew off screaming, as if the shot had been meant for her.

"The next one's in your head, Tyler!" Silver shouted.

Tyler let Raul go.

"Let's try this again," Silver said, calmly. "Get on your belly, Tyler, and put both of your hands behind your back."

Tyler rolled over and put his hands behind his back. Raul tied him up without any problems this time. When he was finished, Silver told Tyler to get to his feet.

During the tussle a few items from Raul's bag had spilled out onto the ground. Raul gathered them up and put them back into the bag.

"Well, colonel," Tyler said. "It looks like you found the mother lode."

"There's nothing here," Silver said.

Tyler laughed. "With all due respect, sir, you're a damn liar!"

"Have it your way, Tyler. Let's go."

Raul led the way, with Tyler just behind him. Silver and I followed.

Tyler didn't say one word during the entire trip back to camp, nor did Silver. When we got there, I called out to Flanna, but she didn't answer. I looked into the tent. It was empty. The shotgun was still leaning outside the entrance.

"She probably took Doc and found someplace to hide," I said, hoping she hadn't gone looking for me.

"I see she didn't take the shotgun, either," Silver said. "She's going to have to get over that one of these days or she's going to get hurt." He said something to Raul and he ran off. "He'll find her."

I looked over to the other side of camp and saw Fred's body. Silver followed my gaze and shook his head.

"First we'll secure our prisoner," he said. "Then I'll bury his friend. Then we'll start packing and get—"

Tyler threw his arm around my neck and lifted me off the ground. In his free hand he held a small pocketknife just below my eye. It was the same knife I had given to Raul. It must have fallen out of Raul's bag during the scuffle, and Tyler picked it up.

Silver looked as shocked as I felt.

"Let him go, Tyler."

"No, sir. And you're not going to shoot me because you'll kill the boy, too. Now, there was a time when that might not have bothered you very much, but I suspect you've gone a little soft over the years."

Silver just stared at him.

"Colonel, if you don't put the gun down, I snap his neck like a twig. You know I can do it because you taught me how."

I saw the frustration in Silver's eyes. He lowered the shotgun to the ground.

"Now step away from it, colonel."

Silver took a few steps backward. Tyler moved forward without releasing his grip on my neck. I couldn't breathe. In one motion he flung me to the side and scooped the shotgun off the ground, bringing it level with Silver's chest.

I glanced at the shotgun by the tent.

"Don't even think about it, son," Tyler said. "Now, just scoot on over there next to the colonel." I got up and walked over to Silver. "I guess this is it, colonel. . . ."

Silver looked at me. "I'm sorry, Jake."

I heard a sharp *thwack* and Tyler dropped the shotgun, staggered, then fell over backward with an arrow sticking out of his chest.

Flanna stepped out from behind a tree on the far side of camp with another arrow already strung in her compound bow.

"Unbelievable," Silver said.

Flanna walked over to us. "Are you okay, Jake?"

I managed to say that I was fine. "How did you know—"

"I heard the shotgun go off. A few moments later, Scarlet came screaming into camp. I figured Silver wouldn't be far behind, so I hid behind the tree."

"With a compound bow?" Silver asked.

"I didn't know whose side you were on," she said.

"Yours," he said. He walked over to Tyler and picked up the shotgun.

"Is he dead?" Flanna asked.

Silver felt for a pulse. "I'm afraid so."

Flanna dropped the bow and started to cry. Silver handed the shotgun to me, then walked over and held her until she recovered.

"How's Doc?" I asked.

"I think he'll be fine if we can keep him horizontal for a few days," Flanna said. "I managed to get him up in the canopy and put him onto one of the platforms so he'd be safe if Tyler came back. When I left, he was yelling at me to give him a rope and let him down, so I guess he's feeling a lot better."

She went on to explain that Doc had regained consciousness the night before. He told her about his dream about Beth being killed in the pit.

"I knew Tyler was headed right for you. I was just about ready to leave and see if I could find you when I heard the shotgun."

Silver looked at her. "I suppose now I'm indebted to you for life or something," he said.

Flanna smiled. "You better believe it."

"There are worse fates, young lady."

We all walked to the tree where Doc was held prisoner. "We're all fine," I yelled up to him.

"Glad to hear it," he yelled back. "Get me a rope and I'll come down."

I looked at Flanna. She shook her head.

"Sorry, Doc. We're kind of busy down here. You just take it easy and we'll get you down as soon as we can."

"I promise I'll take it easy. Just get me down from here. Jake . . . ? Jake . . . ? Are you there? Flanna?"

We walked back to camp.

We buried Fred Stoats and Tyler in the same grave. Tyler would not have been very happy about this, but in my opinion they deserved to spend eternity with each other.

It took us the rest of the day and half the night to pack our gear and get it out to the *Tito*.

By the next morning we were ready to leave. Flanna went off to retrieve Doc and the remaining canopy platform. I went down to the lake and found Silver on the shore, standing in front of a huge pile of maps and old journals.

"What are you doing?" I asked.

"Destroying the trail." He lit a match and dropped it into the pile. He watched the flames for a moment, then reached into his pocket and pulled out the golden jaguar.

"I believe this is yours."

I reached into my own pocket and gave him the second golden jaguar.

"Another gift?" he asked.

I shook my head and told him about the ruins beneath the lake.

"Why don't you keep the jaguars?" I said. "You spent a long time looking for them."

Silver looked at the figurines. "If I keep them, people will wonder where I found them—and maybe they'll come looking. I don't want that to happen."

He smiled and threw them into the center of the lake.

"That's where they belong," he said.

I climbed up to the rock next to the waterfall for the last time. Below me, Silver stared at the burning pile. He looked happy and relaxed, as if he was at peace with himself and the world. It reminded me of the snapshot of him and Tito. He may not have found his son, but it looked as if he had recaptured that same contentment, at least for the moment.

Flanna brought Doc down to the beach. Other than being weak from his illness and irritated at being kept prisoner in the tree for two days, he was in good shape.

Raul took them out to the boat in the Zodiac, then came back and picked up Silver and me.

Silver climbed up to the wheelhouse and started the engine. We heard a loud scream and Scarlet came soaring in from the rain forest. Shore leave was over.

CHAPTER 25

O ur new camp wasn't nearly as nice as the lake camp,
but it was a lot more peaceful.

Flanna set up another web in the canopy while the rest of
us helped Doc catch jaguars. Over the next six weeks we
caught and collared two females. We named one of them
Beth.

Tracking was much more difficult and time-consuming
because we had to do it on the ground. Silver and I took care
of this part of the project, while Raul and Doc conducted a
mammal survey to see what was living in the forest.

While we were having dinner one evening, a small
airplane landed on the river and taxied over to Silver's boat.
We all walked down to the water to see who it was.

The first man out of the airplane was dressed in a white
suit with a white Panama hat on his head. He was rather
short and pudgy and had a white mustache that curled up at
the ends.

"He looks like Mr. Monopoly," I said.

Doc laughed. "In a way he is."

The man walked over to us.

"Jake, I'd like you to meet Mr. Woolcott."

Two other men got out of the airplane wearing conservative business suits, which is not the best attire for the tropics. They looked very uncomfortable. The last person out of the plane was the pilot—Buzz Lindbergh. He looked very comfortable in shorts and a purple tank top. He limped over and gave us all a hug.

"How's the leg?" Doc asked.

"I'm still a little gimpy, but it looks like I'm going to survive! How's the Morpho?" This was directed at me.

"We'll talk about it later," Doc said, quietly. "Let's go up and get Woolcott situated."

All evening long, Doc and Flanna went over the data they had gathered about the flora and fauna of the preserve. The next morning we attached antennas to their airplane. Buzz and Doc took Woolcott for a tour of the preserve as they tracked jaguars.

When they got back, Doc said that he had picked up signals from both Wild Bill and Taw. They seemed to be doing just fine.

"We have to leave early tomorrow morning," Woolcott said. "I'd like to meet with everyone before then."

We gathered together back at camp that evening.

"I'll make this real simple," Woolcott said. "I like what

you've done and I want to fund this preserve. I'll set up an endowment. That way we'll be able to keep it going a long time after we're all dead and buried."

We were all thrilled. Bill's dream had come true.

"Now I assume," Woolcott continued, "that you'll be able to stay on and run it, Dr. Lansa."

"I don't know," Doc said. He looked at me and Flanna. "I was planning to go back to Poughkeepsie."

"We need to talk about this," Flanna said.

AFTER . . .

The recreation room was full. I held the Press Conference after dinner, because I knew it would take awhile to tell the inmates everything that had happened. Well, not everything. I had to leave a few details out, like actually finding the lost mines of Muribeca. If I told them about that, some of the inmates might have checked out of the Home and headed down to Brazil that evening.

When I finished, there were a lot of questions. Over the next few weeks I knew there would be many more.

"What will you do now?" Mr. Blondell asked.

"I have a couple of more weeks of school, then Taw and I are going to take a little trip."

"What about the preserve?" Mr. Clausen asked. "Will you go back down there?"

"Oh, I'm sure I'll go back at some point," I said.

"Is your father going to marry this Flanna girl?" Mrs. Mapes asked.

"I don't know. Maybe someday."

"It's getting late," Peter said. "Jake just got home this morning. He needs to rest."

Taw and I took the elevator up to the second floor. I walked him to his room.

"I'm glad you came back," he said.

"So am I, Taw."

"You'll like Arizona. It's beautiful."

"I'm looking forward to it."

I walked back to my room and looked at the jaguar tooth that Raul had given me and thought about my last night at the preserve.

Flanna had talked my father into staying down there and managing the preserve. Doc said that he wanted me to stay there with him and that he would look into correspondence courses for me.

He was surprised when I told him the next morning that I wanted to fly back to Manaus with Buzz and Woolcott—and from there, catch the first flight back to the States.

"I thought we had it all worked out last night? You're going to stay down here with us."

"I just need to go back for a while," I said. "Taw wants me to go to Arizona with him."

Jaguar

I said good-bye to Silver, Raul, and Flanna. Doc walked me down to the airplane.

"So how long will you be gone?"

"I'll only be gone a month," I said. "Maybe a little longer. . . ."

About the Author

ROLAND SMITH is a research biologist who has been caring for exotic animals for over twenty years. He is also the author of many books for children, including *Sea Otter Rescue, Inside the Zoo Nursery*, and *Journey of the Red Wolf*, as well as the novel *Thunder Cave*, which was named a Notable Trade Book in the Field of Social Studies for 1996. Mr. Smith lives in Stafford, Oregon, with his wife, Marie.